PUFFIN BOOKS

HUNDREDS AND HUNDREDS

Reaching the grand old age of one hundred is certainly an event to be celebrated – doubly so, when 1984 is the centenary year of both the National Society for the Prevention of Cruelty to Children and the Society of Authors.

In honour of this auspicious event, many of Britain's top writers and artists have contributed to this rich and varied collection of new short stories, all taking 'One Hundred' as their theme. There are stories here for everyone: historical adventures, fantasies, science fiction, school stories, fairy tales, sad things and funny things, as well as poems, jokes, puzzles and pictures. *Hundreds and Hundreds* is a wonderful book for 9- to 12-year-olds.

Contributors include: Joan Aiken, John Christopher, Nicholas Fisk, Leon Garfield, Shirley Hughes, Terry Jones, Gene Kemp, Jan Mark, Roger McGough, Philippa Pearce and Jan Pieńkowski, amongst many others, all well known and extremely popular.

All royalties from the sale of this book will go direct to the NSPCC, to help its marvellous and vital work continue for the next hundred years and beyond.

KU-487-566

MARGARET GORDON

HUNDREDS AND HUNDREDS

EDITED BY
PETER DICKINSON

PUFFIN BOOKS

Puffin Books, Penguin Books Ltd, Harmondsworth, Middlesex, England
Viking Penguin Inc., 40 West 23rd Street, New York, New York 10010, U.S.A.
Penguin Books Australia Ltd, Ringwood, Victoria, Australia
Penguin Books Canada Ltd, 2801 John Street, Markham, Ontario, Canada L3R 1B4
Penguin Books (N.Z.) Ltd, 182–190 Wairau Road, Auckland 10, New Zealand

First published 1984
Reprinted 1984

Printed and bound in Great Britain by
Cox & Wyman Ltd, Reading
Set in Linotron Palatino by
Rowland Phototypesetting Ltd
Bury St Edmunds, Suffolk

CONTENTS

and *Gyles Brandreth* all over the place!

INTRODUCTION

The Duke of Westminster

Exactly a hundred years ago, in 1884, the National Society for the Prevention of Cruelty to Children was founded. It was mainly the work of a marvellous man called Benjamin Waugh, who had seen the appalling sufferings of children in London. Tens of thousands wandered the streets homeless, and even those who did have homes were sometimes no better off, because their parents could do what they liked to them and there was no law to stop them.

Thanks to Benjamin Waugh and his helpers, that was changed. Within fifteen years the great Act known as the Children's Charter was passed by Parliament, and for the first time children in Britain had rights better than those of animals.

A great many improvements have been made since then, but the work of the NSPCC will always be vital. Sadly, cruelty cannot be stopped by passing laws against it. In a single year the Society may have to deal with 15,000 new cases. For this work it always needs money, and well over half the money it gets is given by the public. All the profits from this book will go to the NSPCC.

By a happy coincidence 1984 is also the centenary of the Society of Authors, and it was the Children's Writers Group of that Society who decided they would like to celebrate by doing something special for their great twin. This book is the result. I am particularly pleased that it happened like this. A hundred years ago writers, such as Charles Dickens and Charles Kingsley, did much to awaken the conscience of Britain to the sufferings of children, and it is very encouraging for all of us that they should still care.

HUNDREDS AND THUNDREDS

Roger McGough

The sound of hounds
on red sand thundering

Hundreds and thousands
of mouths glistening

The blood quickening
Thunder and lightning

The hunted in dread
of the hundreds running

The sound of thunder
A white moon reddening

Thousands of mad hounds
on red sand marauding

Thundering onwards
in hundreds and thundreds

Thundreds and thundreds
Thundering   Thundering

ONE PENNY – 1884

Marjorie Darke

She was a skinny old bird with stockings in folds round stick legs and wisps of hair sticking from under a greasy headscarf. The pong of her was like old tea and dog, Errol decided. She was on his bus most days when he was travelling to school. Like everyone else he tried not to sit by her, but twice there was no other place. Both times he nipped across the gangway as soon as there was a free space next to his mate, Jas.

'I'd know where you been, even if I hadn't eyes!' Jas pinched his nose. 'By the old witch.'

Errol dug him in the ribs. 'You're nuts! She ain't a witch.'

'Who says?'

'Me. There ain't any witches these days.' He didn't know why he stuck up for her.

That was Monday. Thursday the bus was jam-packed. The old woman was there, and just behind, Jas sitting by Steve Crowson, captain of the under-thirteen cricket team. Errol thought he was a great batsman and inched up the gangway, hoping to stand by them. Then he noticed the only empty seat. As he tried to slide past, the old woman looked up. A smile, wide as a quarter melon, stretched her wrinkly face. Before he could even *think* Bob Marley, let alone say it, he found himself beside her. From behind came a burst of throttled laughter. He felt embarrassed and wanted to tell Jas and Steve to shut it. She'd looked at him as if he was an old friend she hadn't seen in yonks, so what else could he do?

But that wasn't the end of it. She started to talk in a voice that needed an oilcan.

'What's your name?'

'Errol Bowler.' He didn't mind telling anyone his name. A good cricketer's name. He only wished he could live up to it.

'Like cricket do you?' she creaked.

For a split second he thought she was taking the mick. There was another snort of laughter behind. He gave her a fierce stare. She stared back, composed, not mocking. All the same . . . catch him telling her about the way he liked to fancy himself as Viv Richards, walloping sixes out into the road!

'Yes,' he muttered.

'Used to play a bit meself, as a girl.'

Now she was surely stringing him along? Errol studied her face. Dead serious. She meant every word! He was hooked, wanting to hear what else she would say.

'Me dad was a fanatic, see. Used to coach me on our allotment. There was this strip of path between the cabbages. He rigged up a net at the end. He'd bowl – slow, quick, leg breaks, off breaks. I'd hit most of 'em. It was fine till I hit a real flier over a hedge and straight through a greenhouse. Oh my . . . the fuss! You'd've thought it was Buckingham Palace!' She laughed, showing stumps of brown teeth, and Errol laughed with her.

He found himself describing busting a factory window back of his house when cricketing on the waste ground. And how he wasn't allowed to bat in the street since he'd cracked the rear-light on his dad's car.

'Are you in a team at school?' she asked.

It was a sore spot. 'I'm not good enough.'

'Who says?'

He shrugged. 'Mr Sykes . . . the teacher.' Somehow every time old Sykes was scouting for talent, he duffed stroke after easy stroke.

She gave him a long examining look. Then, fishing in the pocket of her tatty coat, brought out something and thrust it into his hand. 'Keep this on you.'

11

The bus was slowing down and Errol, anxious not to miss his stop, found an old-fashioned penny in his palm. Embarrassed, he tried to give it back but she wouldn't accept it.

'Three wishes. You try,' she whispered as if it was a secret between them. Then briskly: 'It's very old. Victoria . . . see? Eighteen eighty-four. Cheerio!'

'Get a move on!' the conductor snapped.

He had to get off. On the pavement Jas and Steve were eager to know what it was all about. He showed them the coin, finding it less easy to explain what she'd said. 'She's loony,' he ended. He felt he'd been had.

'A zoony loony witch!' Jas staggered about, laughing.

'Shut up, man!' Errol almost threw the coin into the gutter, then changed his mind.

They went into school.

By lunchtime Errol thought he might as well try out the coin. Test its powers on something simple.

'Fish and chips!' His mouth watered saying the delicious words.

Finding corned beef salad on his dinner plate was a disappointment but hardly a surprise. Another wish hovered at the back of his mind. He let it come forward before dismissing it as pointless. Then just before the afternoon bell, Jas came pounding over to the house-room to find him.

'Have you seen the notice-board?'

'Why?'

'You,' Jas gasped. 'Twelfth man. Saturday's match against Barley Hill.'

To have his second wish granted before he had properly asked it shook Errol. 'You're kidding!'

'If you don't believe me, see for yourself.'

Jas was right. Standing in front of the school notice-board, Errol read the date, then: 'Westwood v. Barley Hill . . .', his

12

eye travelling down the list to his own name. 'Twelfth man – Errol Bowler.'

It took him all afternoon to believe what had happened. Home at teatime he burst into the kitchen shouting he was in the cricket team for Saturday.

'Why, Errol, that's the best thing I hear today,' his Mam said, setting a plate of fish and chips on the table. 'Get that down you. I've been so busy I ain't had time to cook, so I thought I'd fetch Friday's tea today,' and she laughed.

The time whisked by, with practice in the nets after school both days. Errol had seen the old woman on the bus, but managed to avoid her with no more than a smile. Vague guilt nagged at him until on Saturday he made a decision to sit by her, Monday morning, and tell everything that happened. In the changing-room with the others he put on his whites, slipping the penny into his pocket. One wish left. He trembled on the brink of using it, but pulled back, saving it for emergencies.

The changing-room door opened. Sykes came in. 'Morning you lot. Hope you're all feeling on form. Errol Bowler here? Ah yes . . . well, change your name to Fielder Batsman. Alcott's off sick.'

Errol didn't mind the feeble joke. To have the unwished wish dropped in his lap was a fantastic bonus. He followed the others outside, past the minibus parked near the playing field. The Barleys were tumbling out, clutching bats and pads. Errol felt sorry for their twelfth man.

Steve won the toss and put Barley Hill in to bat. The sun climbed up into the sky as, one by one, nineteen overs were bowled. During the twentieth Errol, at square leg, dropped a catch, letting Barley Hill tot up a final alarming ninety-eight runs. Abandoning caution, he made his last instant wish:

'Let me bat like Viv!'

Between innings he drank some squash, hardly listening to Sykes's pep talk. Sykes and Steve had decided Errol should bat last, so there was a chance he might not be needed. He felt a tiny flicker of doubt.

By twelve o'clock, with a tantalizing score of ninety-five for eight, Steve was stumped, slogging at the first ball of the last over. Errol's stomach tightened. The walk to the crease seemed immensely long. He took guard. The bowler was quick, and the ball came straight at his frozen bat, hit it and trickled away. He gulped; tapped the crease. Waited. This time there was nothing he could do. The ball went wide of the off stump. Three left. He must make some runs . . . *must!*

The fourth ball bounced chest high. Errol jumped up, managing to play it off the splice. No run there. He began to feel desperate. Ball five was mean, and cut in to him, forcing him back towards his stumps. In the nick of time he got his bat down, saving himself from being out l.b.w.

The bowler walked leisurely back. Turned. Errol licked dry lips, concentrating on the final run up, on the round hard shape hurtling towards him. It fell a little short of a length, but measuring the precise moment, with a big swing of his bat he hit it on the up and felt it light as a tennis ball. Not bothering to run, he watched the ball rocket over the bowler's head, away over the fence and into the road beyond.

Six . . . he'd hit a six! One hundred and one. They'd done it! The rest of the team leapt about, cheering, waving arms. Slipping off his glove, Errol felt for the penny.

'Tremendous. Man, you're a knockout!' Jas galloped to him, whacking his back. Then: 'You look as if you've been caught for a duck?'

'It's gone.' Errol's finger poked through the hole in his pocket.

'What?'

'The . . . good-luck penny.' He narrowly avoided saying 'wishing'.

After the cheers and backslaps and handshakes were over, Jas helped him search. They found the penny by a locker in the changing room.

'Must've dropped out before the match,' Jas said.

Errol didn't say anything. Like a slow dawn, understanding came to him. *He* had hit that six. *No outside help*. The implications blew his mind. He couldn't wait to tell the old biddy!

Monday came, with the bus and Jas, but she wasn't there.

He never saw her again.

In 1884

Lizzie Robbins, aged 9:
FLOWER-SELLER

Lives in a basement room with her mother and three younger brothers. Her mother earns 10 shillings (50p) weekly as a factory cleaner. One brother, aged 7, earns 3d a week (just over 1p) running errands. Her father has left home, but occasionally sends the family a little money.

Lizzie attends a Mission school most days. In the evening she buys cheap (faded) violets from a flower-seller in Piccadilly, and then walks round the theatre and restaurant districts, selling bunches at 2½d (1p) each. She returns home about midnight, and gives the money to her mother. A night's earnings average about 8p. FAITH JAQUES

THE POET REFLECTS ON A QUESTION OFTEN ASKED: WHY AREN'T WE ALL HECATONCHEIRES?

(pronounce that word *Heck*-a-tonk-*ai*-rez)

Edward Blishen

1

Lord! fancy being a hecatoncheire!
Imagine waking up one morning and finding the order
   had been varied.
Not: 'Let this person be a human being . . . the usual
   uncluttered design . . .
with an arm or so, and here and there a leg . . .
nothing crowded . . .':
     but instead:
'Let him be a hecatoncheire!'

Awful!

Because it means that you would have a hundred arms,
and so, I needn't point out, four hundred fingers, a
   hundred thumbs,
and more elbows than you'd want
     even if you earned your living nudging people.

There were three of them originally, and quite enough:
Briareus, Cottus and Gyes.
        Early on the scene.
Well, the first Greek gods were Uranus and Gaia, and
    the hecatoncheires were their children.
That's to say, some of their children.
It might be that the idea of two for the sensible number
    of arms hadn't taken root.
But I doubt that. I think the divine imagination was
    playing with the idea that a great number of arms
    would increase one's power.

With a hundred arms you could really get things done.

Some early top brass snapped, 'I've only two hands,
    you know . . .'
and realized that, coming from a god, that was a foolish
    complaint.
Even a divine designer is rash to whine at his own
    design.
'Then do something about it!' was what some other
    immense creature must have muttered.

The more arms the better!

And heads. Have I said that each of the hecatoncheires
    had fifty heads?

Concentrate for a moment on the idea of your head
    being turned into a crowd.
Imagine the simple amazement of having a hundred
    ears!
You'd become a piece of human radar, switching
from ear to ear, along the path of your obviously
    enormous shoulders.

Fancy having to be in command of fifty expressions on
    fifty faces!
You'd need a control-board for all the smiles and smirks
    and sneers!
Of course, you could send a grimace rippling down the
    row and back again –
or arpeggios of protruding tongues.
But would it be worth it?

And imagine at school – 'Take those grins off your
    faces!'
The question might be: *Which* faces?

2

But it's the hundred arms that bother me.

At school, again, they'd say: 'Do me a hundred lines!'
Then they'd look twice and say: 'Make that a million!'

Imagine losing a glove!

The fellow you're down to fight is smaller than you,
so they all cry: 'Leave him alone!
        or fight him with ninety-nine arms behind your
    back!'

'Tell me,' the teacher says, 'the reasons for and
    against . . .
oh, the width of the Amazon basin, the Treaty of Tilsit,
    the life-cycle of a fly . . .'
'On one hand,' you begin: '. . . and then on the
    other . . .
and the other . . . and the other . . . and the other . . .
    and the other . . .'

'Two million lines for taking all the afternoon
        over a simple question!'

'I'd give forty-five of my right hands,' you'd groan,
'not to have to do those lines!'

At cricket they'd make you face fifty simultaneous
    bowlers,
simultaneously sending up a mixture of bouncers,
    googlies, offbreaks and plain yorkers.

'Every half-day in the nets, child – you need to get your
    hands in!'

And in the woodwork room, whilst the rest did
    handicrafts, you'd do handsicrafts,
and be required to produce a hundred small,
    uneven-legged stools
or the same number of little boxes, not absolutely
    closeable
(nor, after being used once or twice, quite openable!)

I plunge my heads in my hands at the thought of it!

3

Do you feel, as I do, an enormous complacent pleasure
in the idea of having arms, two: heads, one?

All the same, I expect you wonder why it didn't catch
    on.
Why, after three, they discontinued the line.

The fact is that when the Titans, who were cousins of
    the hecatoncheires, were fighting Zeus,
the king of the gods, they thought they'd won.

How would you trap the almighty except in an even
   almightier net?

Which is what they did.

But Briareus was sent for, with his four hundred clever
   fingers, and one hundred supple thumbs,
and turned that terrible net into a terrible tangle of
   string.

And I imagine Briareus felt he had made a point.
About the usefulness of being hundred-handed, I
   mean.

But work it out for yourself!

4

There were just three hecatoncheires, and that was the
   end of it!

BRANDRETHISMS

Toss a coin in the air 200 times. The chances of the coin landing
heads up 200 times in a row are slight. In fact, the odds are
16069380442558990275541962092341162602552220299378279283501375 to 1 against you.

Amazing, isn't it?

If you lived for a million seconds, you'd only live for 12 days. If
you lived for a billion seconds, you'd live for over 31,000 years.

Amazing, isn't it?

GYLES BRANDRETH

WHO'S AFRAID?

Philippa Pearce

'Will my cousin Dicky be there?'

'Everyone's been asked. Cousins, aunts, uncles, great-aunts, great-uncles – the lot. I've told you: it's your great-grandmother's hundredth birthday party.'

'But will Dicky Hutt be there?'

'I'm sure he will be.'

'Anyway, Joe, why do you want to know?'

Joe's mother and father were staring at Joe; and Joe said, 'I hate Dicky.'

'Now, Joe!' said his mother; and his father asked: 'Why on earth do you hate Dicky?'

'I just do,' said Joe. He turned away, to end the conversation; but inside his head he was saying: 'I'd like to kill Dicky Hutt. Before he tries to kill me.'

When the day of the birthday came, everyone – just as Joe's mother had said – was there. Relations of all ages swarmed over the little house where Great-grandmother lived, looked after by Great-aunt Madge. Fortunately, Great-grandmother had been born in the summer, and now – a hundred years later – the sun shone warmly on her celebrations. Great-aunt Madge shooed everyone into the garden for the photograph. The grown-ups sat on chairs, or stood in rows, and the children sat cross-legged in a row in the very front. (At one end, Joe; at the other, Dicky; and Dicky's stare at Joe said: 'If I catch you, I'll kill you . . .') There was a gap in the centre of this front row for a table with the tiered birthday cake and its hundred candles.

And behind the cake sat Great-grandmother in her wheel-chair, with one shawl over her knees and another round her shoulders. Great-aunt Madge stood just behind her.

Great-grandmother faced the camera with a steady gaze from eyes that saw nothing by now – she had become blind in old age. Whether she heard much was doubtful. Certainly, she never spoke or turned her head even a fraction as if to listen.

After the photograph and the cutting of the cake, the grown-ups stood around drinking tea and talking. (Great-grand-mother had been wheeled off somewhere indoors for a rest.) The children, if they were very young, clung to their parents; the older ones sidled about aimlessly – aimlessly, except that Joe could see Dicky always sidling towards him, staring his hatred. So Joe sidled away and sidled away . . .

'Children!' cried Great-aunt Madge. 'What about a good old game? What about hide-and-seek? There's the garden to hide in, and most of the house.'

Some of the children still clung to their parents; others said 'yes' to hide-and-seek. Dicky Hutt said 'yes'. Joe said 'no'; but his father said impatiently: 'Don't be soft! Go off and play with the others.'

Dicky Hutt shouted: 'I'll be He!' So he was. Dicky Hutt shut his eyes and began to count at once. When he had counted a hundred, he would open his eyes and begin to search.

Joe knew whom he would search for with the bitterest thoroughness: himself.

Joe was afraid – too afraid to think well. He thought at first that he would hide in the garden, where there were at least grown-ups about – but then he didn't trust Dicky not to be secretly watching under his eyelashes, to see exactly where he went. Joe couldn't bear the thought of that.

So, after all, he went indoors to hide; but by then some of the best hiding-places had been taken. And out in the garden Dicky Hutt was counting fast, shouting aloud his total at every count of ten. 'Seventy!' he was shouting now; and Joe had just looked behind the sofa in the front room, and there was already someone crouching there. And there was also someone hiding under the pile of visitors' coats – 'Eighty!' came Dicky Hutt's voice from the garden – and two children already in the stair-cupboard, when he thought of that hiding-place. So he must go on looking for somewhere – anywhere – to hide – and 'Ninety!' from outside – *anywhere* to hide – and for the second time he came to the door with the notice pinned to it that said: 'Keep out! Signed: Madge.'

'A hundred! I'm coming!' shouted Dicky Hutt. And Joe turned the handle of the forbidden door and slipped inside and shut the door behind him.

The room was very dim, because the curtains had been drawn close; and its quietness seemed empty. But Joe's eyes began to be able to pick out the furnishings of the room, even in the half-light: table, chair, roll-top desk, and also – like just another piece of furniture, and just as immobile – Great-grandmother's wheel-chair and Great-grandmother sitting in it.

He stood, she sat, both silent, still; and Dicky Hutt's thundering footsteps and voice were outside, passing the door, and then far away.

He thought she did not know that he had come into her room; but a low, slow voice reached him: 'Who's there?'

He whispered: 'It's only me – Joe.'

Silence; and then the low, slow voice again: 'Who's there?'

He was moving towards her, to speak in her very ear, when she spoke a third time: 'Who's there?'

And this time he heard in her voice the little tremble of fear: he recognized it. He came to her chair, and laid his hand on hers. For a second he felt her weakly pull away, and then she let his hand rest, but turned her own, so that his hand fell into hers. She held his hand, fingered it slowly. He wanted her to know that he meant her no harm; he wanted her to say: 'This is a small hand, a child's hand. You are only a child, after all.'

23

But she did not speak again.

He stood there; she sat there; and the excited screams and laughter and running footsteps of hide-and-seek were very far away.

At last, Joe could tell from the sounds outside that the game of hide-and-seek was nearly over. He must be the last player not to be found and chased by Dicky Hutt. For now Dicky Hutt was wandering about, calling: 'Come out, Joe! I know where you're hiding, Joe, so you might as well come out! I shall find you, Joe – I shall find you!'

The roving footsteps passed the forbidden doorway several times; but – no, this time they did not pass. Dicky Hutt had stopped outside.

The silence outside the door made Joe tremble: he tried to stop trembling, for the sake of the hand that held his, but he could not. He felt that old, old skin-and-bony hand close on his, as if questioning what was happening, what was wrong.

But he had no voice to explain to her. He had no voice at all.

His eyes were on the knob of the door. Even through the gloom he could see that it was turning. Then the door was creeping open – not fast, but steadily; not far, but far enough –

It opened far enough for Dicky Hutt to slip through. He stood there, inside the dim room. Joe could see his bulk there: Dicky Hutt had always been bigger than he was; now he loomed huge. And he was staring directly at Joe.

Joe's whole body was shaking. He felt as if he were shaking to pieces. He wished that he could.

His great-grandmother held his shaking hand in hers.

Dicky Hutt took a step forward into the room.

Joe had no hope. He felt his great-grandmother lean forward a little in her chair, tautening her grip on his hand as she did so. In her low, slow voice she was saying: 'Who –' And Joe thought, He won't bother to answer her; he'll just come for me. He'll *come* for me . . .

But the low, slow voice went on: 'Whoooooooooooooooooo –'
She was hooting like some ghost-throated owl; and then the
hooting raised itself into a thin, eerie wailing. Next, through
the wailing, she began to gibber, with effect so startling – so
horrifying – that Joe forgot Dicky Hutt for a moment, and
turned to look at her. His great-grandmother's mouth was
partly open, and she was making her false teeth do a kind of
devil's dance inside it.

And when Joe looked towards Dicky Hutt again, he had
gone. The door was closing, the knob turning. The door clicked
shut, and Joe could hear Dicky Hutt's feet tiptoeing away.

When Joe looked at his great-grandmother again, she was
sitting back in her chair. Her mouth was closed; the gibbering
and the hooting and the wailing had ceased. She looked
exhausted – or had she died? But no, she was just looking
unbelievably old.

He did not disturb her. He stood by her chair some time
longer. Then he heard his parents calling over the house for
him: they wanted to go home.

He moved his hand out of hers – the grasp was slack now:
perhaps she had fallen asleep. He thought he wanted to kiss
her goodbye; but then he did not want the feel of that century-
old cheek against his lips.

So he simply slipped away from her and out of the room.

He never saw her again. Nearly a year later, at home, the
news came of her death. Joe's mother said: 'Poor old thing . . .'

Joe's father (whose grandmother Great-grandmother had
been) said: 'When I was a little boy, she was fun. I remember
her. Joky, then; full of tricks . . .'

Joe's mother said: 'Well, she'd outlived all that. Outlived
everything. Too old to be any use to herself – or to anyone else.
A burden, only.'

Joe said nothing; but he wished now that he had kissed her
cheek, to say goodbye, and to thank her.

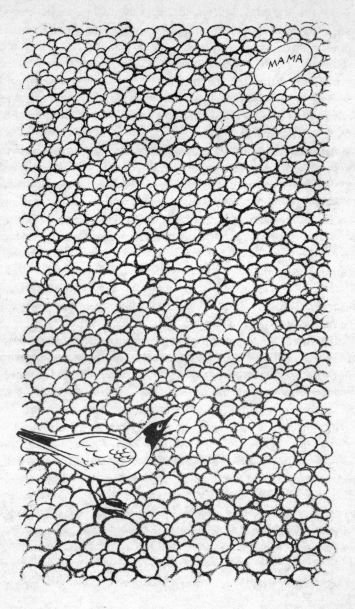

Hundreds of pebbles   PAULINE BAYNES

UMPTEEN HUNDREDS

Helen Cresswell

Archie Harris was a self-made man. Well, perhaps more a self-made lad – he was still only nineteen. He had a silver Rolls Royce and a gold-plated Porsche. He had computers that could do everything short of contacting the Martians, and his own private helicopter. He had made his fortune designing and producing garden gnomes.

'No garden is complete without its Archie Harris Gnome,' said his latest advertisement, which showed a clump of these knobby, highly coloured objects on the terrace of a well-known stately home. (Even a duke cannot afford to turn down the kind of money Archie Harris offered. It was rumoured that he had even approached the Queen, who, for the time being at any rate, thought she *could* afford to turn him down.)

Archie Harris had gone from rags to riches in three years flat. He would have admitted himself that it was just like a fairy tale – if he had known what a fairy tale was. The TV set at 14 Carter Terrace had been turned on more or less non-stop since the day he was born. There had certainly never been any books, or bedtime stories.

The only thing Archie was now lacking was a home of his own. He still lived with his parents in Wapping. He enjoyed whizzing about the world selling his gnomes to the Arabs and Chinese, and staying in five-star hotels, but still liked being at home best. Mrs Harris's steak and kidney pie and apple turnovers were unbeatable. Lately, however, he had become restless. The real trouble was that there wasn't enough room to house all his stereo equipment and records.

The truth was that what Archie secretly fancied was a

palace, and the trouble with *that* was that palaces are very thin on the ground. Also, they are usually already occupied – by queens, dukes and such.

One weekend when there wasn't much on TV Archie decided to go out and look for a palace himself.

'I'll take the helly,' he told his parents. 'I'm off on a reccy. I'll find somewhere this weekend, or bust!'

'We love having you at home, Archie, we do really,' his mother said. 'But the dusting is getting to be a bit of a job with all your records and stuff.'

'I've told you, Ma, I'll buy you a mansion,' he replied.

'And I've told *you*, Archie, that your pa and I don't *want* a mansion,' she said. 'You can only watch one TV programme at a time, no matter *how* many rooms you've got!'

'OK, OK,' said Archie. 'Bye!'

He stepped into his Rolls Royce and drove off to his helicopter pad. If there *were* any palaces hidden away in deepest Surrey, then he reckoned he should be able to spy them out from the air.

He enjoyed flying the helicopter. It was his next favourite thing after watching the telly. He was soon out of London and over the countryside, dotted here and there with the odd mansion, but not a sign of towers and turrets. Then, all at once, he found himself flying into a dense cloud – a dense *pink* cloud. He was surprised, but not staggered. Over the years he had seen a fair number of pink clouds on the telly adverts. When he came out of it, he saw a dense forest, stretching as far as the eye could see.

'Could it be the New Forest?' wondered Archie.

His geography was not particularly good. Then he saw something that *did* make his eyes stretch.

'A – a palace!' he exclaimed. 'A blooming palace!'

And so it was, a palace all of white, with gold-tipped towers winking in the sun.

'Just like Walt Disney!' Archie breathed, enchanted.

He brought the helicopter lower and saw a wide, paved courtyard, ideal for landing. Archie did not hesitate. (He had not made his millions by hesitating.) Down he went and set the helicopter down in the centre of the courtyard and switched off the engine. The blades whirred to a standstill. Archie sat gazing at the palace of his dreams. 'This feels like home,' he decided.

Patiently he sat and waited to be surrounded by the astonished occupants of the palace.

'I'll put in an offer they can't refuse,' he thought, and mentally arranged clusters of his gnomes on the terraces. It did occur to him that the place, on closer inspection, looked run down, to say the least. Everything was overgrown, by roses mostly. There were roses everywhere, even, he noted with growing mystification, across doorways.

'The folks must be away at their *other* palace,' he decided. 'In Monte Carlo, or somewhere.'

He climbed out and stood for a moment in the blazing courtyard. The only sounds were the occasional whistles of birds and the murmuring of bees. The longer he stood there the more uneasy he felt. Archie Harris was not used to peace. What he was used to was an eternal background of television or pop music.

He walked towards a high, arched door that stood slightly ajar and was fastened only by a network of briars. A man was sitting crosslegged against the wall, his eyes closed, mouth ajar.

'Morning!' said Archie loudly.

No reply.

'Morning!' he shouted.

As there was still no reply Archie felt justified in stirring the sleeper with his foot.

'Something rum here,' he thought. 'Rum set of clothes he's

wearing, as well. Don't see gear like that around much – specially nightcaps, with pompons.'

He even had a sudden wild thought that what he was looking at was not a human being at all, but a new type of life-sized garden gnome. His heart thudded.

'Could be a whole new thing!' he thought. '*Life*-sized, for the top end of the market! Dukes, and that – earls! Dead lifelike it looks, as well! It's a real good paint job!'

Archie was now possessed by a fresh excitement. Not only had he found his dream palace but also, it seemed, a promising new sideline in garden gnomes. First on the agenda, however, was to look the place over.

He had to struggle with the climbing roses first. This took some time. Archie was not a very physical person. His main exercise took the form of pressing knobs and switches. At last the door swung open with a loud, reverberating creak, just like the ones in the late-night horror movies. Archie, who had no ambition to encounter Dracula, or a werewolf, or such, peered cautiously in.

'Good grief!' he exclaimed.

The June day had gone to fog. All was grey, blind, blurred. He took a bewildered pace forward, and squeaked. He clawed at his face and pulled away a softly clinging film.

'Cobwebs!'

The fog was of cobwebs, vast and sweeping beyond all dreams of cobwebs. They fell fold upon fold from ceiling to floor. Archie was not very physical, but he was not a coward, either, and was in any case by now in a fever of curiosity. Slowly he moved forward, hands outstretched like a sleepwalker, pulling at the dusty veils as he went. He could make out the blurred outlines of what seemed to be human shapes. These proved to be further life-sized gnomes in a variety of poses.

'Indoors!' thought Archie. 'That could be a whole new area

of development! Life-sized gnomes for the garden *and* the house! *Very* upmarket! A-shoo! A-shoo!'

Dust flew. Archie valiantly sneezed his way forward and fell headlong on some unexpected steps. He raised himself up and saw, incredulously, a king gnome and a queen, seated on tarnished thrones.

Archie Harris was out of his depth. Even now he did not recognize the scenario. In his childhood, he and his parents had been too mesmerized by the silver screen to bother with fairy tales. But he had not made his millions by turning back in the face of a challenge. He sneezed his way onward until he reached the foot of a winding, spiral staircase. Onward and upward our hero went.

'A-shoo! A-shoo!'

At the top he groped his way through a further succession of giant webs. He stopped. There before him was a fourposter bed, and on it lay what looked like the figure of a girl, sleeping. Archie craned forward.

'That's no gnome!' he decided. If it were, then a fortune awaited the manufacturer. The skin was pearly, faintly flushed, the lips were parted. Golden hair spilled over the pillows. She looked just like the girl on the TV advert, the one who goes in slow motion along the beach while her hair flies out in long, shining, undulating waves.

'Blimey!'

Archie stared at the sleeping shampoo girl. Then, seized by an irresistible impulse, he leaned over and kissed her on the lips. This was a very uncharacteristic act. Archie had never bothered much with girls, and had never, in fact, so much as kissed one. Making his millions had been a full-time job. Even so, he knew that the lips he had just kissed were not those of a gnome. He found the experiment so agreeable that he was about to repeat it when the shampoo girl stirred. She murmured drowsily and stretched her arms and the dust flew and 'A-shoo! A-shoo!' sneezed poor Archie.

Her eyes opened. They gazed straight into Archie's own. Then, 'My prince!' she whispered.

Archie, confused as he was, was quick to deny this.

'Oh no!' he exclaimed. 'Archie Harris.'

Her look was bewildered.

'Of Archie Harris Garden Gnomes,' he added modestly. 'Will you marry me?'

He clapped his hand to his mouth. The words were out before he could stop them – they were out before he had even meant to say them. It was as if he were speaking lines learned for a play.

'Oh my prince!' she sighed. 'I will!'

Archie leaned over and kissed her again. He was interrupted by the sound of excited voices and a renewed billowing of dust that set him unromantically sneezing again.

'Briar Rose! Briar Rose!' came voices out of the fog. 'Darling daughter, where are you?'

It was some time before the dust settled and everyone could see everyone else. Bit by bit Archie grasped what was happening. He, it seemed, had just awoken the girl from a hundred years' sleep by kissing her on the lips. She was not, it appeared, the girl from the shampoo advert, but a princess called Briar Rose. And the stout parties in crowns who were now beaming at him like adverts for gravy seasoning were the King and Queen – his prospective father- and mother-in-law.

If only Archie had known his fairy tales he might have cottoned on sooner. As it was, he was still in a fog, in every sense of the word. He was used to chairing board meetings and running multi-national companies, but the confusion in the newly woken palace had him truly flummoxed. All the life-sized gnomes had miraculously come to life and were running hither and thither, greeting one another with screams of excitement and raising prodigious clouds of dust. The Princess had disappeared – probably to shampoo her hair and rinse away a century of dust. Every now and then someone would come up to Archie and wring him painfully by his hand. The word 'wedding' was on all lips.

Archie was somewhat alarmed by this. He had been thinking rather on the lines of a suitable period of engagement (during which the palace could be cleaned up and fully computerized), followed by a wedding at St Margaret's, Westminster, or even, given his bride's pedigree, the Abbey.

Feeling himself to be something of a spare part, he wandered from room to room, looking for a TV set. He did not find one. He became aware, with mounting unease, that there seemed to be no electrical, let alone electronic, equipment in the place. When he stumbled into what was evidently the kitchen and found a whole ox being turned on an open spit, and plucked turkey feathers flying everywhere, panic set in.

'I'll radio HQ and get some equipment flown in,' he decided. He had not become a multi-millionaire at the age of nineteen without being able to keep a cool head in a crisis.

In the courtyard he found his helicopter surrounded by a group of gaping and yawning courtiers, all unshaven and cobwebby. A stir ran through them as he approached, just in time to see a tiny, hunched figure, all in black, scuttle from the cockpit and scoot away like a disturbed spider. He did not recognize this figure as the wicked fairy. To him it resembled something that, on a TV advert, would be tackled with an aerosol spray.

Archie pushed his way through the distinctly smelly crowd (who could also, he thought, benefit from the use of an aerosol spray) and climbed into the machine. He let out a sigh of relief as he settled into the familiar seat. For two pins, he thought, he would take off, there and then. He had, it was true, found the palace of his dreams, and a princess to go with it, as a bonus.

But the whole scene was so depressingly out of date that the prospect of modernizing it was daunting. He hardly even liked to think what the Electricity Board would make of it. But he stiffened his spine. Archie Harris never turned his back on a challenge. He saw himself rather as the hero of the TV advert for a power cleanser, sweeping all before him. He would stick to his original intention, and radio for supplies.

The snag was that the ignition key had gone. Archie stared blankly at the empty slot in the dashboard. His gaze then moved to the crowd of courtiers.

'Now then,' he said sternly, 'who's got it? Who's taken my key?'

They shook their heads.

'We have not set foot in your windmill,' one greybeard said. 'What a very strange . . . er, interesting windmill it is, sire.'

'*She* took it!' shrilled a small page. 'I saw her! That wicked old godmother!'

This remark gave Archie pause. He knew about godfathers. He'd seen the movie at least three times. But god*mothers* . . .

He climbed moodily down from the helicopter. As he did so, he caught sight of that tiny black figure in a doorway, beckoning.

'I must negotiate,' he told himself.

Seen close to the creature was so unprepossessing that had Archie had an aerosol spray to hand he would have been tempted to use it. He stared coldly at the long chin, hooked nose, glittering eyes and toothless leer.

'You have the Princess,' she crooned, 'and I have – this!'

A tiny claw, clutching the key, stabbed out from the black folds of her robes and as swiftly disappeared.

'I'm going to marry the Princess, as a matter of fact,' he told her loftily. 'And I'm going to live here. I'm going to do the place up. Not before time, either. It's a disgrace. But I'm used to challenges. I'll soon have the whole place so computerized that its own grandmother wouldn't recognize it!'

The creature remained silent, the leer fixed.

'Did you hear me?' he demanded. 'Don't you understand?'

'Oh, I hear,' she replied. 'It is *you* who do not understand. You with your whirling bird out of the sky – I saw you come, I saw you!'

Archie kept his cool.

'I'll trouble you for the key of that "whirling bird" as you call it,' he told her. 'It's a helicopter, for your information.'

'Oh, you shall have it,' she said, 'at a price.'

Archie had been prepared for this. As a matter of fact he quite enjoyed haggling over prices.

'OK,' he answered. 'Name it, and we'll talk.'

'The Princess, Briar Rose,' said the crone.

Archie stared.

'What d'you mean?'

'I mean another prick on the finger from the spindle, another hundred years.'

This, to Archie, who had vaguely heard of the Sleeping Beauty, but did not know the story, was gibberish.

'Listen!' she hissed. 'Briar Rose has been woken before, many, many times. *And* by proper princes, who hacked their way through the forest and thicket in a proper manner. *They* didn't cheat – *they* had no whirling birds. But there was always something they didn't understand. And I don't think you do, either.'

'What?' demanded Archie.

'That when she fell asleep,' said the crone softly, 'time in the palace stood still. A hundred years may pass in the world outside, but not here. Not a single second passes here, once her eyes close.'

Still he stared.

'When she first fell asleep was so many hundreds of years ago I can't remember how many. *Umpteen* hundreds. And only when a prince wakes her with a kiss do the clocks start ticking again. And when her suitors discovered that they, too, would have to go back to the beginnings of time, they changed their minds, every one of them. No man likes to go back. You all want to go forward, always forward! It's called Progress – and *that*'s the real curse that lies on Briar Rose! I'm doing her a kindness when I put her back to sleep every time.'

'You mean to say,' said Archie, 'that we're not in the twentieth century?'

'Nowhere near,' she returned, 'and never will be, for many a long century.'

'Let me think a minute,' said Archie. His head was spinning. What she seemed to be saying was that the palace would *never* have electricity – not in his lifetime, at any rate. No electricity, no TV, no stereo, no computers . . . the prospect was a nightmare. No Princess, even if she *did* look like the girl in the shampoo advert, could ever, possibly, be worth it.

'In any case,' he told himself, 'I owe it to the world to get back into the twentieth century. Where would it be without Archie Harris Garden Gnomes?'

He did not hesitate. Those who hesitate do not make millions.

'You're on!' he told her. 'In fact – thanks for telling me. I thought the whole deal was too good to be true.'

The crone held out her skinny palm and Archie took the key.

'Better go now,' he said. 'Quick!'

Briar Rose had a lot of hair, and no hair drier, but one never knew. She might come tripping out of the palace at any moment and make an embarrassing scene.

'You're sure she'll be all right?'

'Certain. I told you. She's been sleeping now for umpteen centuries. Another century will be neither here nor there.'

36

'You're right,' he said. 'Well – cheers!'

Archie Harris strode back across the courtyard, through the cluster of courtiers and into his helicopter. The propellers whirred and the courtiers screamed and threw up their hands and ran helter skelter back to the safety of the palace. Archie grinned, and the next minute was high above the trees. He took one last look at the white, gilded pinnacles of the palace of his dreams, and headed back for London, and the twentieth century. He re-entered the pink cloud.

It was several days before the helicopter was found, lodged at the top of a high tree in a wood near Surbiton. Of Archie Harris there was not a sign. But in the cockpit was a lot of dust, and some ancient bones that experts said were at least a thousand years old. They could not, of course, have been the remains of Archie, Mr and Mrs Harris knew that. All the same, they were all there was, and so they took them home and buried them in their garden in Wapping. Above it they erected a life-sized garden gnome, as a memorial. There was no epitaph.

This was a pity. The fate of Archie Harris could have served as an awful warning to others. There should have been an epitaph reading 'Those who know their fairy tales never, ever trust a witch.' Or 'Witches Rule. OK?' Something like that.

YET ANOTHER BRANDRETHISM

Two people playing dominoes for ten hours a day and making a move every fifteen seconds could continue playing for 118,000 years without exhausting all the different combinations of dominoes possible in the game.

Amazing, isn't it?

GYLES BRANDRETH

THE BORROWER

Patricia Miles

There were five children in the family, Mary, Kate, Maurice, Michael and James, and of the five Kate felt sure that she was the most unfortunate. Why was she the one her mother had chosen to run an errand for Mrs Dignam, *again*? Kate must have run hundreds of errands for Mrs Dignam. Hundreds and hundreds, and without so much as an apple, let alone a few sweets, by way of thanks. Not that Kate was a greedy child. True, she had a liking for sweets, but she wasn't mad for them. No, it was just that, like most children, she had a well-developed sense of fair play. And it simply wasn't fair to keep sending her great long errands to the Creamery – three miles, there and back! – with no reward at all.

She laced her boots with a sulky look on her face – this was in the days when children wore boots, and their mothers wore

DO YOU KNOW **WHY** THE GRAND OLD DUKE OF YORK

MARCHED HIS TEN THOUSAND MEN

ALL THE WAY **UP** TO THE TOP OF THE HILL

long awkward skirts of serge that swept the floor, and the girls had white pinafores, and hair in plaits, which in the case of Kate's twisted when they should have hung straight. She muttered as she bent down, 'I'm sick of going her errands.'

'What's that?' Her mother was inclined to be severe, and Kate could be defiant.

'Nothing, mother.' What was the use? When you were always told to be polite to the neighbours. In a small farming community such as theirs that was one of the most important rules, and Mrs Dignam – and her easy-going husband – were their next neighbours along the lane.

Mrs Dignam had married late in life and had no children of her own. That was why she was forever borrowing Kate. It wasn't all she borrowed. She was a mean woman and she borrowed in a mean way. It was almost an art with her. She would come in the evening – when it was too late to buy anything – and then ask, with apologies and smiles, for the tiniest little loans possible: 'just half a cup of sugar, Ellen' – this was the children's mother – or 'a few spoonfuls of tea', or 'a wee bit of black thread to sew a button on', all such small items

VAL BIRO

she surely could not be expected to return them – though she easily could have.

'What have I to get this time?' Katy asked.

'A three-pound bag of cooking salt and a pair of mended shoes.'

Oh *no*. Why was it always something heavy and awkward to carry?

'Can Mary come with me?'

'No. She has the geese to bring in.'

They all had jobs to do. It was only a small farm, but fertile, and if everyone worked who could work, they could manage. Kate knew that really, and plodded off alone, burdened with her colossal sense of injustice; wishing too that she had blue eyes like her sister's china doll, and dark hair like Michael's, instead of her own carroty red – because if you were going to be fed up you might as well be fed up about everything.

'Did she give you the money?'

She had reached the Creamery, or rather the fine general store attached to it. Here farmers could buy what they wanted and either pay or have it balanced against the milk they brought in.

Kate handed the manager the Creamery book. 'She said to put it down.'

He was a cheerful young man in a blue striped shirt, and he whistled as he fetched the mended shoes and made them into a parcel with the salt, and jotted down the cost. All this time Kate was gazing at the shelf behind his head – crammed with sweet jars from one end to the other.

'Is that all, the salt and the shoes?'

'Oh, and twopence worth of sweets.'

He looked up at her, surprised.

She had very nearly surprised herself. This was no calculated crime; it was the prompting of the moment. Good or bad? She hadn't time to sort it out – he was speaking again.

'Are these for Mrs Dignam?'

'No, they're for me – for going so many errands.' Her voice sounded peculiar, and she could feel a blush rising – from her ankles, as it seemed to Kate. He must know she was lying. The manager himself looked like a figure in a distorting mirror, the kind she had seen, once, at the seaside. Very strangely, he winked. He didn't say anything but he winked – and filled in the tuppence. At least, she thought he winked; and in any case she chose gloriously – humbugs, pear drops, treacle toffee and fruit bon bons – you got a lot for tuppence in those days.

Kate could hardly wait to get away with her prize. She hurried gleefully up the lane, telling herself how glad she was and how clever she'd been. Then she stopped and opened the bag. Oh what joy, what satisfaction there would be in that first sweet! And indeed the first one did taste truly delicious. She had chosen a humbug; she was saving the pear drops for Maurice, her friend. And some for Mary? No – Mary would give her away. So would the little ones, without meaning to. She munched her way through a few more. She had really more than, in the circumstances, she could manage. She thought of throwing them away then, but her pride wouldn't let her. She trudged on. She was on the last stretch now, and her mind began flinging up daft, hopeful images of the outcome. Mrs Dignam wouldn't check the book. She would check it, but she wouldn't mind. Transfer of parcel from right arm to left arm. She'd always *meant* for Kate to have a few sweets. Of course, that was it! Nearer home now. She ate a treacle toffee, thoughtfully. She would have liked to save something for her mother – her mother liked fruit bon bons. Was she *mad*? If her mother ever found out – she would *kill* her! She ate another

41

humbug. Trudge trudge, munch munch. Strangely cloying and unattractive that humbug became. Queer hot and cold feelings ran all over her and her heart thumped in a sickly fashion. And here was the Dignams' farm.

There was no one about, only the old dog and he knew her. She crept quietly into the kitchen, put the parcel on the table and made off.

Maybe nothing would happen at all.

The evening passed. The jobs were done, the little ones were in bed and the lamp was lit. Their father was out, somewhere. Their mother was sewing, making, or rather re-making, clothes. Mary was mending socks. They sat in the kitchen by the range, Kate pretending to read and listening to the slow tick-tock of the clock. 'You're safe. You're safe. You're safe,' said the clock. But oh, thought Kate, would bedtime never come?

A hand tapped at the window.

'Can I come in?' A head appeared around the kitchen door.

'Come in, Janet, come in.'

Mrs Dignam came fully into view; in her hand she had the Creamery book. 'There's a little mistake here, Ellen. Look, look, you can see: twopence, and against it, in this column, he's written "sweets"!' Her glance slid from the page, towards Kate. Kate trembled.

'I see,' said her mother, with amazing calmness. 'Come here, Kate. Was this your idea?'

Kate nodded, speechless with fright.

But in the same calm tone her mother continued: 'I think, Janet, you've rather made use of the child – and her shoe leather – but she has done wrong. Hand me my purse, child. You shall have the twopence back.'

From Kate's point of view, there could have been no better

answer. But Mrs Dignam took it as a rebuke, which indeed it was. She took it well.

'Oh no, no,' she cried. 'She's a good child. I wouldn't think of it.' Her hand made a small move forward to take the coppers, then drew back. She smiled apologetically and turned to go. Then, as she reached the door – 'I wonder, Ellen,' she said – 'I'm very low for washing soda; could you spare me a small handful?'

Their mother didn't hesitate for a second. 'Well, Janet,' she said. 'It just so happens I can let you have a whole new packet – you can give me one back when you're ready. Run and get it for me, Kate.' And Kate did.

In 1884

Henry John McNaughton, aged 11:
PAPER-DELIVERY BOY

The eldest of three children, Henry lives with them and his mother in one room. Father's whereabouts unknown. Henry's mother earns 10 shillings a week (50p) as a charwoman in a private house, and can occasionally bring home left-over food.

Henry attends a Board School, which costs 9d weekly (about 3p). He does one paper round before school and another at night, and earns 3d (just over 1p) a day. This pays for his schooling, and his mother has the rest for the upkeep of the family.   FAITH JAQUES

THROUGH THE CENTURIES

Peter Dickinson

Three generations go to a century,
So *your* great-grandfather could have seen Victoria
And your fifteen-greats-grandmother might have met
   Elizabeth
And your thirty-greats-grandfather been bonked by
   the Conqueror
For getting in his way when he came here
   conquering.

If you were a fruit-fly things would be different –
One generation's less than two weeks for them.
So *your* great-grandmother was born last holidays
And your thirty-thousand-greats was chomped by
   the Conqueror,
Sitting on a strawberry he ate without noticing.

Looking at it that way, it's no great mystery
Why little fruit-flies aren't taught history.

*Oh well,
here today,
gone tomorrow!*

M.13 IN FORM ONCE MORE

Gene Kemp

*Told by X who never dares to give his/her name. The Cat's revenges
are terrible and timeless.*

'Books is comin',' yelled Mandy the Boot, blundering into
the classroom in her father's size 12 army boots and knocking
Slasher Ormeroyd flying, which caused him to leap up with a
mad roar and lurch to attack her, except that the Cat (Felix
Delaney) paused in the middle of a poker game with Lia Tansy,
Chinky Fred and Tom Lightfinger to call out, 'Cool it,
Slasher,' so that he hauled back his huge maulers, for he
always does what the Cat tells him. As we all do.

'What books?' enquired the Cat gently, for he was a great
reader: crime and horror.

'A crateful. Old Perkins is turning 'em over an' oinkin' like a
ma pig with piglets. There's at least a hundred.'

'Mr Pertins has comed back to us, doody, doody,' crooned
Daisy Chain, blue eyes beaming, bright hair bobbing. She
loved Mr Perkins, and he was fond of her, not that he had
much choice, M.13 not being noted for its lovable characters.
Mind you, we were all pleased to see him. He'd been absent on
a course and the teacher they sent instead left in tears on
Wednesday morning, making the rest of the week very tedi-
ous. The Headmaster took us. His name is Mr Bliss and it's a
lie.

'That's great,' said Bat Pearson, resident genius. 'And about
the books. We need new ones. Not that I read much fiction,
haven't the time' – she was wading through *A Study of Bog
Burial in Scandinavia and Europe* (funny place to bury people,

said Mandy) – 'but I like to keep Killer going and he can't stand *Little Women*.'

Killer, six feet two and growing, nodded, for Bat does all his work. In return he's her Minder. Most of us need one. M.13 isn't popular in the school, not that it's popular out of it either.

'I like Enid Blyton,' cried Hot Chocolate, the class prefect. 'I've read them all. Sir once said they'd made me what I am.'

'Yeah,' growled Mandy the Boot, 'fascist, sexist and racist, which in your case especially is disgusting.'

'Speak for yourself,' shrieked Lia Tansy, the Cat's woman, she of the golden skin and golden eyes.

'Belt up,' bellowed Hag Stevens from the doorway, 'Mr Perkins is on his way.' We were all so pleased to see him that we arranged ourselves nicely, looking keen and eager. And instead of sighing as he usually does at the sight of us, he smiled, which smoothed out all his wrinkles like an American with a face-lift.

'It's so nice to see you all again,' he said warmly, and as if that wasn't enough he was dressed in cords and check shirt. Where was his old chalky? What was up?

'As you know, I've been on a course, a language course, which I really enjoyed, and now I feel we can go forward with a new outlook.'

'A wha . . . ?' asked Brain Drain, dim even by M.13's standards.

'A new outlook on the rest of our year together. Speaking to you honestly, as your friend as well as teacher, that course came just in the nick of time, for I'd begun to despair at the thought of us struggling and drowning together . . .'

'I wunt let yer drown, Sir,' interrupted Brain Drain, breathing hard, for more than two words was difficult, 'I kin swim.'

'Quite,' Sir agreed. 'Now let's see if my old friends are all here . . . Abdullah, Asra, Brian . . .'

Killer and Slasher were despatched to carry in the heavy crate, Bat, Lia and Mandy to organize the class resource centre. The rest of the school has a central area, but it was decided that M.13 should just keep theirs in the classroom, after Tom Lightfinger flogged all the cassette players and musical instruments to some teenage pals to start a group.

'Any 'orror comics or girlie mags?' Slasher asked Killer hopefully.

'No, shurrup. The Cat looks after that side, and y'know he don't think it right for old Perkins to learn about such things. Not at his age.'

Eventually all the splendid new books were arranged and the classroom transformed. Mr Perkins had done well, something for everyone: Dr Seuss for Brain Drain and Daisy and The Heap, *War and Peace* for Bat, *An Anthology of Horror* for the Cat. He beamed at us all.

'Yes, you shall soon get at them, but first something new for a new day. Has anyone a poem for me? A suitable poem, mind, Ormeroyd.'

A mind-boggling hush fell for we always turned to the Cat or Bat or Mandy to represent us on these occasions and they all three despised poetry (wet, useless, boring). And then Brain Drain lumbered to his feet.

'I know one about an ickle worm.' And he recited it while Sir grinned like a maniac.

'Jolly good,' he cried. 'They told me it would work. Good old M.13. Don't let me down. Surely you must know a poem, Beatrice.'

Bat stood up, grimacing horribly, embarrassed. 'The only one I know is a dead boring one from Horace, about a smelly, skinny youth. Dates back to my classical hang-up last year. Sorry. Will that do?'

Sir nodded, and the Latin phrases hung in the classroom already quite well known for its language. Killer smiled

47

approvingly. His Bat was doing well even if no one could understand a word of it. And Tom Lightfinger got up, brick red. 'Know one about a dicky bird,' he said, head down. 'Learnt it in the Infants.' One by one M.13 made their offerings, the Cat last, with the lyrics of an obscure cult rock group.

A week later anyone walking into M.13's classroom, and most people preferred not to, would have had to weave their way through poems everywhere – on the walls, on the windows, standing in displays, hanging on string, swinging in mobiles, for M.13 had taken to poetry, writing poems, reading poems, reciting poems, illustrating poems. Mr Perkins had seen a miracle in his lifetime and walked on air. The school grapevine had it that the class had either gone barmy or had reformed at last. Actually it was, as usual, the Cat.

Shoulders hunched, black glasses, white face, he said,

'I want old Perkins happy. De poetry makes him happy. So we get with de poetry. See?' We saw.

When it wasn't poetry, it was stories. M.13 went book mad, reading all of the time all over the place, even walking round the playground reading with Killer and Slasher ready to settle anyone foolish enough to find it funny. Those who understood what those squiggles on a page meant helped those who didn't.

So occupied were we, we didn't notice that the school's big issue was now Conservation. A famous celebrity had addressed the school on the subject and projects mushroomed everywhere. But it wasn't until a very pretty lady came to tell the school of the plight of a butterfly that was about to die out unless money could be raised to provide a Nature Reserve where it could breed that M.13 realized it was needed.

'Dat poor ickle 'utterfly,' muttered Brain Drain, moved.

Now despite everything – lies, thefts, vandalism, dishonesty, cheating, bullying, greed, truancy, you name it, M.13's got it – despite all these or as well as, M.13 has Heart.

Disasters, they weep over disasters. Earthquakes bring contributions from them faster than anyone. Tom Lightfinger has been known to pinch the Save the Children bottle from the corner shop to contribute to the class's gift. So when the very pretty lady said there was to be a prize for the best school contribution – a silver medal – and a framed poem about a butterfly written by the very pretty lady herself for the best class collection, there could be no doubt about it. M.13 intended to get that prize, that poem on their wall.

No one needed to tell M.13 about fund-raising. They have a natural talent for it: begging, gambling, sponsoring, busking, collecting, blackmailing, grovelling, stealing, shop-lifting, extorting, bullying, even selling, they went about it all in the way that suited each of them best. Yet in the final week but one, the grapevine informed the Cat that Hadley Grove School were the favourites, their rich parents being plushier than ours.

Mr Perkins was heard to remark with pleasure on the industry of his class, most pleased, most pleased. Reading, writing and money-raising thrived. An experienced teacher, though, every Friday he collected in the books that had worked the miracle (he thought) and checked them. That Friday only Bat's was missing and she promised faithfully etc. Mr Perkins went home. Happy.

On Monday morning all the shelves were empty. All the books had disappeared. So had every leaflet, magazine, poster and map in the resources area. His face sagged back into all those wrinkles as he took the register, all present, except for Brain Drain.

'Right, what have you lot done with them?' He didn't look at all like that nice Mr Perkins. He looked more like Hanging Judge Jeffreys.

'Delaney, what have you organized?'

'Nothing, Sir,' the Cat at a loss, for once, 'honest.'

'You don't know what honesty is, Delaney.'

But the Cat stood firm; it was nothing to do with him nor anyone else that he knew about.

'Then Lightfinger, it just has to be you.'

'No, no, no. I liked the books. They just took what I was half-way in the middle of and I haven't finished. And I dint read the ending first, for once.'

'Hard luck,' snapped Mr Perkins, cruelly.

And the door crashed open as the vast, shaggy head of Brain Drain appeared, then the rest of him, waving a fistful of money.

'For de 'utterfly pome, Mr Perkins. For de pome. We win it now, won't we? Look at all de lolly. And I did it for you, Mr Perkins, becos you give me all dem pomes and I love pomes now.'

'Brian, look at me and stop gabbling. Where did you get that money? And do you know what's happened to all our books?'

'I've conserved our books. Dey'll go on f'ever an' ever. An' dey gived me lolly for 'em. Look.'

'But how?' groaned Mr Perkins.

Brain Drain was panting like an old train at full steam ahead. 'Me Auntie Mave. Cleanin' after school, an' she give me this dustbin bag an' I put 'em all in an' took 'em to our church for rebikin' . . .'

'For what?' Mr Perkins looked as if he was going demented.

'Recycling,' translated Bat.

'An' they said what a good cause, and gived me money an' we'll win the pome now, wun't we?' he beamed. He sat down and then bobbed up again in the heavy silence. 'Mr Perkins, Sir?'

'Yes, Brian?' came a low moan.

'I conserved them books and the 'utterfly, dint I?'

'Oh, Brian, you did, you did.'

After a long time the Cat spoke, and for possibly the first time in his life, his voice was full of pity.

50

'M.13. Listen. De kindness, get it? From now on we are going to be kind to Mr Perkins.'

How M.13 later visited the recycling plant, rescued all the books (not very suitable anyway, they said), was spotted by the Mayor, also visiting, got its picture in all the papers (such keen children), won the school medal and the butterfly poem (more pictures in the papers – what fine, hardworking children, an example to others) so that at last Brain Drain could hang the pome on the wall – except they'd gone on to computer games by then – and as usual were hated bitterly by the rest of the school (good, hardworking, boring children) is another story.

In 1884

Millie Pearson, aged 10:
MATCH-SELLER

Lives in two rooms in Lambeth, with her parents and four younger brothers and sisters. Two other children died in infancy. Her father, a skilled carpenter, earns 29 shillings a week (£1.45). Millie attends a charity school, and sells matches outside the pubs near her home on summer evenings and Saturdays. The matches are long-headed 'fusees' and sell at one penny (less than ½p) for a box of twenty.

In the winter Millie helps her mother at night with sewing and mending for private customers.

FAITH JAQUES

Hera was married to Zeus the greatest of the gods. He took a fancy to Io, and he turned her into a cow to mislead Hera, who then demanded Io as a gift.

Argus, a two-faced giant, was employed by Hera to keep an 👁 on Io ✳ ✳ ✳ ✳ ✳ Zeus then sent his son Hermes to kill Argus and free Io. ◦—◦—◦—◦—◦

But Argus had a hundred ◉ s, and only fifty of them slept at a time. So Hermes played music until all hundred eyes slept. Then he cut off Argus' head.

Hera was very sad at the death of poor Argus and had his hundred eyes transplanted into the tail of her peacock. Io ran away ***

THE CENTURION

Clive King

'Fish?' the Captain growled. 'Who's going to cook them?'

I don't know what they called him in his foreign army but we called him the Captain. He was pacing up and down the dusty courtyard and he'd hardly looked at the fish I'd brought. I stared at him, as I stood in the sun with the flies buzzing round the fish basket on my head.

'My brother will cook the fish, Captain sir,' I said.

'Your brother's gone sick too,' said the Captain.

Oh no, not my brother! It was hot but I got a cold feeling in my belly. Half the Captain's men had gone down with this sickness and some of them had died.

The Captain went on pacing and muttering. He can't have been talking to me so he must have been talking to himself.

'A hundred men to keep the peace! Half of them sick – and now it's the cook. I'd rather spare the other fifty.'

Of course he was right. What would the Captain do without my brother? Any fool can cook for a soldier, but my brother was more than a cook to the Captain. He was the one who knew everyone in our town, knew where to find everything the Captain wanted. How could fifty soldiers keep the peace, or even a hundred? But the Captain and my brother were doing their best.

'You're a mucky little urchin,' the Captain was glowering at me. 'But your brother's a good lad. Better go and see him.'

I carried the fish into the kitchen and covered them with a damp cloth. Then I went into the little room where my brother slept. He was lying on the little low bed, moaning, with the sweat streaming off him. I took the mug from his bedside,

54

filled it with fresh water from the kitchen, and tried to get him to drink it. He didn't seem to know I was there. He looked like death.

I went to the doorway into the courtyard and waited for the Captain to pace in my direction.

'Captain sir!' I said.

'What is it?' he barked.

'Please may I go for the doctor, sir?' I asked. 'I will find money to pay.'

The Captain got quite angry with me. 'You don't think I'd let him just lie there, do you? Doctor's been and gone. And a lot of good that did!'

I stood unhappily in the doorway as the Captain paced away and back again. But an idea had come to me.

'Captain sir! May I send for the healer?'

The Captain stopped pacing.

'What's that?' he barked.

Well, I didn't know much about this healer myself. All I could say was, 'He – he makes people better, sir.'

'That'll be a change,' said the Captain. 'Go and find him then.'

So off I went. On my way out I nearly bumped into an important-looking man coming in. It was the Mayor of our town. He looked at me as if I wasn't there.

I didn't know where I was going, but I had to do something. I was fond of my grown-up brother, and he was all the family I had left. If he died I would be out of a job too. Nobody paid me for the fetching and carrying I did, but – you know, some of the marketing money stayed in my pocket.

I wished my brother was with me to help, but of course he couldn't be, could he? It was the sort of errand he enjoyed doing. You don't know who you're looking for or where he lives, but you've got to find him. I'd have to manage on my own. I went down to the market, where I knew people.

There was a stall that sold herbs and perfumes and medicines. I asked the merchant if he knew where I could find the healer.

'Healer?' the merchant said suspiciously. 'There's some sort of quack going round the mountain villages. But you keep clear of him, lad! He won't do *us* no good.'

The mountain villages. At least that was a start.

There was a woman with live hens to sell, their legs tied together with string. I could tell by her dress that she came from the mountains. I asked her if she knew about the healer – and I'd struck lucky. She went off on a long story about her cousin who'd been a cripple for years, and how this healer had come along and now her cousin was back to work as a woodcutter. 'A bit stiff still, now and then, you know how it is, especially of a damp morning –'

'Where is he now?' I interrupted her.

'My cousin? Well, he's living with my uncle still, of course –'

'Not your cousin. The healer. Where can I find him?'

She didn't know. But she gave me the name of the village where her family lived. And if she'd walked from there with her chickens it couldn't be far off.

So I set off up the mountains. The winding roads take a long time, but if you know the right footpaths and the dry watercourses there are plenty of short cuts. They are much steeper, though, and I'm a towny, not a mountaineer. My legs were soon aching, and I was puffing and panting in the hot sun. I sat down under a pine tree to get my breath back.

A boy came along with a herd of goats and I asked him the way to the village. He pointed over the other side of a steep ravine and said I'd have to go down to the bottom and up again. He laughed at me, but I could have cried, after all the climbing I'd done. He asked me why I wanted to go to that village anyway and I told him I was looking for the healer.

He laughed at me again, and I nearly hit him. But he pointed the other way up the mountain.

'The healer's up that way,' he said. 'Why didn't you ask?'

He seemed to be pointing at nothing but a steep cliff.

'Is there a path?' I asked.

'A goat path,' he said. 'Come on, I'll show you.'

We and the goats scrambled up the narrow path across the face of that cliff. I didn't dare look down. When we got to the top there was the made-up road leading to a village. But the road was blocked by sawn-off treetrunks, and a handful of armed men were lounging by the barrier. And there was the important-looking man I'd seen at the Captain's house! What was he doing there, and how had he got up so quickly? Of course he must have had fast transport to take him up by the road, while I was sweating up the mountainside.

The Mayor was standing on our side of the barrier, arguing with an armed man on the other side. Don't ask me why the road was blocked off, or who the armed men were. You never knew in these mountains.

The Mayor was waving his hands in the air. 'But it is an important request from the Captain in the town!' he was shouting.

The other man lifted his own shirt away from his chest with fingers and thumbs. It meant: *This shirt doesn't touch my chest: your request doesn't touch me.*

The Mayor changed his tune, his hands swimming, palms upwards.

'Look, my friend,' he wheedled, smiling. 'We don't care much for your healer. But we want to do the Captain a favour, see? The Captain's a good man. We got a lot of money out of him to rebuild our meeting-house. Someone's told him about this healer and he's sent for him.'

The guard lifted his weapon and poked it into the Mayor's

broad belly. The Mayor went pale, turned round, and came back along the road, fuming. Of course he didn't notice me sitting by the roadside, in despair. This important busybody had taken on my errand, and botched it. But if he couldn't get through, what chance had I got? I'd come all this way for nothing.

But all this time the goats had been nibbling their way along the bank of the road towards the barrier. The armed men took no notice of them, and they didn't even seem to see the goat-boy. He picked up a dry stick and handed it to me.

'Prrtt!' He made a loud noise with his lips and tongue to the goats. I got the idea. I waved my stick and tried the prrtt noise too. The goats drifted along the bank above the barrier. The goat-herd and I drifted past the barrier after them. The armed men took no notice. We were part of the landscape, like the rocks and the almond trees.

I smiled at the goat-herd and made for the village. There seemed to be a lot of people about, gathered in the orchards, sitting or standing quietly with their backs towards me. In the middle of them all someone was speaking. I went up to a woman with a baby on the edge of the crowd, touched her on the arm, and asked, 'Is it the healer?'

She looked round, put her finger to her lips, and said, 'Shh! He's speaking.'

I tried to listen to the words, but they didn't seem to have much to do with me, with my mind on my sick brother. The speaker told one or two good stories, though, and it was cool and peaceful up in the mountains, and I sat and rested.

Then the words came to an end and people started moving, and I pushed my way into the middle of the crowd. There were quite a few people there with crutches and bandages and sticks, but I pushed through them too, though somebody tried to stop me. There was the healer with his back to me. My heart was thumping in my chest again, like when I was climbing the steep slopes.

I tugged at the healer's shirt sleeve.

'Please sir!' I said. 'Please come and heal my brother. Down at the Captain's house in the town. He's dying of the fever.'

The healer turned and gave me a long careful look. People pushed me aside, but I heard the healer's voice. He just said, 'I'll come.'

I heard people telling him not to go down to the town, that it wasn't safe and so on. But somehow I knew that he meant what he said, and – it seems silly but I felt as if my brother was better already. I just had to get down the mountain and tell him so.

Going downhill's only too easy, but you have to stop yourself going too fast. I'd had quite a few tumbles by the time I got to the bottom, and my knees and elbows were scratched and bleeding. When I got to the Captain's house I went straight to my brother's room. He was lying under a blanket in the stuffy place, shivering so much that his bed was knocking against the wall. But his eyes opened, and he knew me. I gave him some water and said, 'It's all right, the healer's coming.' And his shivering died away and he closed his eyes in sleep.

I thought I'd better tell the Captain about the healer coming, so I looked for him in the courtyard. He and another man were sitting in chairs, drinking wine or something. *Oh no!* It was that important-looking Mayor. He was there ahead of me again! I skulked behind the leafy vine to hear what he was saying.

'There's something I must tell you, my dear Colonel.' That *colonel* bit was just flattery, and they both knew it. 'He's one of their holy men, this healer. I decided it wouldn't do to have him in the town, let alone your own house. It would only disturb the peace. I'm sure he wouldn't come anyway.'

I was raging behind the vine leaves. The old *liar*! He hadn't decided anything. He'd been scared off by the armed men. And what did he care if my brother died? My rage drove me out into the middle of the courtyard, in front of the two men.

'The healer's coming!' I shouted at them. 'He's coming to make my brother better. He's coming because I asked him!'

The two men looked at me standing there, with my torn clothes and scratched knees. I didn't know what else to say. It was the Captain's house, after all. And the Mayor's town.

And just then a soldier came in from the street, stood stiffly to attention, and saluted the Captain.

'Beg pardon, sir. Checkpoint reports a group wanting to pass through. Some kind of medical person, one of them says he is. Not the usual doctor, sir. But he says he's invited here.'

There was a silence, and then the soldier added, 'Sergeant says, sir, he doesn't look the type of person you *would* invite –'

'That'll do!' The Captain cut him short.

There was another silence. You could see the Captain thinking. In the army you have to make up your mind quickly. When he spoke it was to me, not to the Mayor or the soldier.

'Boy, you invited him, you can take a message back to him. Be sure you're polite and respectful, d'you hear? Say he's a holy man and I'm a hard-drinking soldier, not fit to have him under my roof. But say I know what it is to give an order. *Quick march*, and off they go! *About turn*, and back they come! Know what I mean? Tell the cook to do something, and he does it. Same with your healer. He gives the order – your brother gets better. Off you go.'

I wasn't happy, but you can't argue with a man like the Captain. I went off with the soldier into the darkening streets.

When I got back I went straight to my sick brother. I whispered in his ear, 'Listen! The healer says you're to get better.' My brother smiled in his sleep.

Then I went to the Captain. He was sitting alone, still drinking.

'Well?' he asked gloomily. 'Did you give him my message? What did he say?'

'He laughed, Captain sir,' I replied.

The Captain scowled at me.

'*Laughed?*' he demanded. 'I thought he was one of your solemn holy types. What d'you mean, *laughed*?'

'He thought it was funny, sir,' I said. 'He said you were the only one here who believes in him.'

My brother did get better. And with luck we'll have the Captain here for keeps.

In 1884

William Jones, aged 10:
CROSSING-SWEEPER

(A hundred years ago the roads were cobbled or dirt-surfaced, pot-holed and puddled. All vehicles were drawn by horses or donkeys, so the roads were very dirty, and crossing-sweepers were an important part of town life.)

William shares a pitch across a busy shopping street with his brother George, aged 11. Every pedestrian who uses their crossing gives a halfpenny tip. In bad weather the boys can earn 10 shillings (50p) a day, in good weather much less.

William and George should attend school, but never have. Neither can read or write. Their father is dead and their mother abandoned them. At night they sleep in a ramshackle empty house, with a tribe of other homeless boys.

FAITH JAQUES

LEGENDS OF ST THICK

Peter Dickinson

This year we celebrate the centenary of the Blessed St Thick. We might as well, because the exact year of the saint's birth is not known. He himself could never tell how old he was, being unable to count beyond four. (His thumb confused him.) Because ordinary people found it easier to identify with St Thick than with other men of great holiness and learning, many legends are told of him. Here are a few.

St Thick and the Devil

One evening the Devil came to St Thick and offered to make him clever. St Thick was sorely tempted, but he had been cheated so often by men taking advantage of his simplicity that he at last learnt a thing or two.

'What's in it for you?' he asked.

'Just my usual fee,' said the Devil. 'Sign here.'

And he produced a pen and a bottle of special ink, stronger than dragon's blood, made from the brimstone cinders of the pit.

'I cannot write my name,' said St Thick.

'Then make your mark,' said the Devil. 'That will do.'

St Thick dipped the pen in the ink, but not being used to pens he dropped a great blot on the document, just where the words were written signing his soul away.

'Fool,' said the Devil. 'I'll have to write it all again.'

To cover his embarrassment the saint looked around for something to drink. Seeing the ink-bottle he picked it up and swallowed the contents, the Lord miraculously hardening his gullet for the purpose. By this time the Devil was in such a rage that St Thick thought he had better make his mark to pacify him, so he picked up the pen and with the last ink on it made the only mark he knew. Not a $\times$ but a $\dagger$. This caused the Devil to disappear in a puff of sulphur.

'That was good strong liquor,' said the saint.

St Thick Saves Rome

Attila the Hun was on his way to sack Rome when he met St Thick, praying by the wayside. St Thick was only on his way to the next village, but he had forgotten the road and was praying for guidance. Seeing a harmless stranger, Attila the Hun, as was his custom, lifted up his great club and smote the saint on the skull, intending to bash his brains out. But such was the marvellous thickness of the saint's cranium that the club splintered into a hundred pieces. Deeply impressed, Attila the Hun ordered the saint to guide him to Rome, but St Thick had a slight ringing in the ears after the blow and thought he was asking to be taken to the saint's home.

Now, as it happened the saint had just set up home in a commodious cave, unaware that a large and savage bear was hibernating there. He ushered Attila the Hun into the cave just as the bear woke up and came lumbering out, looking for a good meal. That was the end of Attila the Hun, and so the Holy City of Rome was saved from sack by the miraculous stupidity of St Thick.

St Thick Discovers America

The Pope decreed that the lack of learning of certain holy men was a scandal to the Church, and to set an example he commissioned a hundred learned scholars to teach St Thick the rudiments of the Faith. They taught him for a year and a day, working in shifts, and at the end of that time he was not a comma wiser. So the Pope, to remove the scandal, told St Thick to go and convert the heathen. Obediently St Thick went down to the shore and found two short planks, which he lashed together and made a raft. The wind blew him from shore, and he was lost to sight.

A year and a day later he returned, saying that he had sailed to a great land, where the people had copper skins and wore great feathered head-dresses and signalled to each other with smoke and a lot of other absurd and incredible stories.

'But did you convert them to the Faith?' said the Pope.

'I taught them everything I knew,' said St Thick.

'That won't have taken long,' said the Pope, in his scornful pride.

But it is well to remember that St Thick had discovered America, which was more than that Pope could say for himself.

St Thick and St Thomas

St Thomas Aquinas, as everyone knows, was the wisest man ever. No knowledge in all the world was beyond him, or so he thought. In the pride of his great learning he set out to search the world and see if there was anything he did not know. He travelled through all the lands of Christendom and found nothing, so he started for home. On the last night of his long journey he put up at an inn and by chance he found St Thick, who had gone there hearing the singing and mistaking it for a place of worship. The saints fell into conversation. All night St Thomas studied the different facets of the ignorance of St Thick, and as the sun rose he fell on his knees and said, 'I have been saved from a great sin. I thought I knew all that could be known, but I do not know how it is possible for a man to be so stupid as this holy brother.' And he blessed St Thick and bought him a pint of wine and went humbly home.

When St Thick died and came to the gates of Heaven, he stood and stared at the infinite jewelled walls and the glittering pinnacles and all the holy spirits like different coloured flames moving among them. He fell on his knees, ashamed of his stupidity, and let the other dead souls crowd by. As he knelt there his eye fell on a pebble – nothing but a pebble, fallen from the shoe of some pilgrim. He picked it up and began to turn it over in his palm.

Evening came, and St Peter was about to shut the gate, when he saw the old man kneeling in the dust, gazing at something in his hand.

'What have you there, friend?' said St Peter. 'And aren't you coming in?'

'Oh, it's just a pebble I picked up. An amazing thing is a pebble.'

'We have wonders much greater than that to show you inside,' said St Peter. 'You must be very easily amazed.'

'Oh yes, I am,' said St Thick. 'I think, sir, the wonders of heaven might be too much for me. I am better off with my pebble, wondering at the roundness of it, and the greyness of it, and the hardness of it, and that it should exist at all.'

'No doubt it was put there for you to find and think about,' said St Peter. 'My brother, you know something that the wisest of men do not always know. Come in. You will not be ashamed.'

So St Thick went through the gates, and the angels sang for him and he understood their song, and his pebble was set in the midmost point of the Throne, where a space had lain waiting for it since before time was.

Which witch spied a spider? Which spider spied a witch?

PAULINE BAYNES

THINK OF A WORD

Joan Aiken

Once there was a boy called Dan who was in the habit of using short rude words.

Almost any short word ending in T was rude in the country where Dan lived: Dit, Fot, Het, Rit, Sut.

'You silly old Sut,' he called after an old lady in the street one day, and she turned round on him, quick as a whiplash.

'You'll be sorry you said that to me,' she said.

'Why, you old Jot?' said Dan.

'Because, from now on,' said the old lady, 'every time you say one of those words you seem so keen on, a square inch of your skin will turn to glass, so that everybody will be able to see all the works inside you. There are eight words that would cure the habit you have,' she said, 'but *I* shan't teach them to you. You'll have to find them out for yourself.'

And she turned on her skinny old heel and walked away.

Dan was left standing there with his mouth open.

He didn't call anything after the old lady – somehow she had left him rather quiet and thoughtful – but, later in the day, he forgot all about her, and called the driver of the school bus a stupid Nat.

'Coo! Dan!' said his friend Rod who was sitting beside him. 'Your face has gone all funny! I can see your teeth through your cheek as if it was glass. *And* the buttermint you're sucking. You didn't tell *me* you had any buttermints.'

Dan, quite upset, couldn't wait to get home and look in the mirror.

Sure enough, a patch of his right cheek had gone clear and

see-through – there were his teeth and his tongue, plain to view.

It was like having a plastic porthole in his face.

And, after two or three days, a good few more patches had gone transparent all over Dan – on his arms, his legs, his neck, and even more inconvenient places. You could see bones and muscles in him, and tubes and joints and things that aren't usually seen.

The family doctor was quite keen to send Dan up to a big teaching hospital, so that the medical students could look at him and find out useful facts. But Dan's mother wasn't having any of that.

She was very annoyed about it, and so was Dan's father.

'It's disgraceful,' they said.

So, since Dan couldn't seem to stop coming out with short rude words ending in T, they took him away from school and sent him off into the mountains to be a shepherd.

Up high in the hills, alone all day with the sheep, he couldn't come to much harm, they reckoned, as there was no one to talk to, and so he wouldn't be using any language, and, by and by, might learn to think before he spoke.

So off went Dan, into the high meadows, where he had no company but the baaing sheep and a surly old dog called Buff, who never barked, and who made it plain to Dan that he could have looked after the whole flock perfectly well on his own, without any help.

There, sitting on a rock, or on the short, sweet mountain grass, Dan had plenty of time to think, and to wonder which were the eight words the old lady had meant.

Day after day he thought, week after week, and he never spoke.

Thoughts piled up inside his head like leaves in a hollow tree. He thought about how you could tow away the wind, if you had a strong enough rope. He thought about how, if you laid your plans carefully, you could win summer or winter to be your very own. He thought about rolled and stuffed thunder, and pan-fried lightning. He thought about weaving a rope of rain. He thought about the air, which is everywhere. He thought about the earth, which is nothing but a shepherd's pie of everything left over.

Words are stronger than blows, he thought. And perhaps, he thought later on, thoughts are stronger than words.

So Dan passed days and weeks and months, wandering among the hills with his sheep. He was happy now. He didn't even want to go back to his home.

He listened to what the wind had to say, he watched the dark and the light playing hide-and-seek with each other, he felt the rock under his toes, he tasted the rain and smelt the warm salt wool of the sheep.

Meanwhile, down in the plains, and in Dan's home town, they were having a lot of trouble with dragons.

Dragons had suddenly started breeding quicker than wasps, and the whole country was full of them. Put your Sunday joint in the oven, and half an hour later a dozen dragons would have smelt it out; they'd be battering at your window like bulldozers.

Dragons fouled up the airport runways with claw-marks and scattered scales and droppings; they burst into banks and snatched bags of cash; they came snorting into cinemas and burned up reels of film; they broke off TV aerials and scraped tiles from roofs; splashing in rivers they turned all the water to steam; they swallowed down hundreds of men, women and children going about their daily affairs. And as for princesses – there wasn't a single princess left free in the world, for the dragons had collected the lot, and had them all shut up together in a nasty, greasy, cindery castle, which stood on an island in the middle of a lake, up among the highest peaks of the mountains, which in that part were so tall and sharp that they looked like the spikes of a king's crown.

Dan knew nothing of all this.

He did notice, to be sure, that dragons flew overhead much more than they used to: all of a sudden there would be a big spiny shadow across the sun, and the sheep would bleat in fright and huddle together, and old Buff the sheepdog would growl and snake out his head with flattened ears.

Dan noticed, too, that knights and princes and soldiers were quite often to be seen, riding horses or tanks or motorbikes up the highways into the mountains. From his perch on a high crag Dan would see them go up, but he never saw them come down again. Up, up, the tiny figures went, and vanished into the high passes. Maybe they were crossing the mountains to the other side, Dan reckoned. He didn't give them too much thought. Nor did he trouble his head about the distant rumblings and flashes from those high peaks where they went. A bit of bad weather in the mountains was nothing out of the common. The sheep didn't mind it, nor did Dan.

But one day a young fellow in shining armour, a handsome lad with a ruby-hilted sword and a gold crown around his helmet, came riding past the crag where Dan sat with his flock.

'Good day, shepherd!' called the knight. 'Am I going right for the dragons' castle?'

Dan had to work his jaws and his throat and his tongue for quite a few minutes before he was able to answer – so many months had it been since he had spoken last.

'Umph – dragons' castle?' he croaked out at last. 'Dragons' castle? I'm not sure I know of any dragons' castle.'

'Oh, come *on*! You must know of it! Where they have a hundred princesses shut up together inside – and a hundred dragons on the rampage outside. You mean to say you live up here in the mountains and you haven't heard of that?'

'I mind my own business,' croaked Dan.

But when the knight told him that the castle clung like a cork in a bottle to the tip of a steep island in a mountain lake, Dan was able to set the knight on his right way.

'Up the pass, keep left, round a mountain shaped like a muffin – that'll take you there.'

'*You* seem to live here safe enough, shepherd,' said the knight, rather surprised. 'Aren't you afraid for your flock, with so many dragons about?'

'They can't land here. The slopes are too steep,' Dan told him. 'A dragon needs a flat landing strip, or a stretch of water. Or a crag that he can grab hold of. Slopes are too slippery for them.'

All this Dan brought out very slowly. Finding the words was hard work, and tiring, like a walk through deep mud.

'I can see that you know a lot about dragons,' the knight said, looking at Dan with respect. 'I wonder – can you suggest any way to deal with them?'

'Dragons don't trouble me,' mumbled Dan.

'No – but when I meet one of them – what should I do?'

Dan began to wish that the stranger would go away and leave him in peace.

'Oh,' he said quickly – anything to get rid of the fidgety young fellow – 'just write a word on your forehead with the tip of your finger dipped in morning dew. If you do that, then you'll have power over the dragons.'

'Well, fancy, now!' said the knight. 'What word should I use?'

So Dan quickly told him a word, and he set spurs to his horse and shook the reins. But then, pulling back, he turned and called, 'Don't *you* want to come and rescue those hundred princesses?'

Dan shook his head, and the knight galloped away up the pass.

Sitting down again, Dan gazed at his flock, peacefully nibbling and munching. What? Rescue a hundred princesses? Not likely! Just think of the chattering and giggling and gabbling – the very thought of it made his head buzz. But still, he wished good fortune to the young knight. And now he began to feel a trifle anxious and bothered; for the advice he had given was thought up quite hastily on the spur of the moment. The words had come into his head and he had spoken them. But he hadn't the least notion in the world whether the idea would work or not.

Maybe I ought to go after that young fellow and tell him not to try in case it doesn't work, he thought. Only, if I did that, who would keep an eye on my sheep?

Buff opened one eye and gave a bit of a growl.

What's troubling Buff? Dan wondered. Are there more strangers about?

And then he turned round and noticed a skinny old lady perched near by on a ledge of rock. Quite comfortable, she looked, and as if she had been there a good long time.

'Found out the use of words, have you, then, Dan?' said she cordially. And Dan answered her right away, as if the answer had been tucked away in a cupboard of his mind, waiting for this moment:

'Trees are swayed by winds, men by words.'

'Right,' said the old lady, nodding her head energetically. 'And now you've learned that, don't you forget it, Danny my boy. But,' she went on inquisitively, 'what was the word you told that young fellow to write on his forehead?'

'That was a word for *him*,' said Dan. 'Not for any other.'

'Right again,' said the old lady, nodding some more. 'Words are like spices. One is better than a hundred. Learned a bit of sense, you have. Remember it, and maybe you'll be some use in the world by and by.' With that she vanished, like a drop of water off a hot plate, and Dan picked himself a blade of grass and stood chewing it thoughtfully, looking at where she had been.

Next morning early, Dan heard a distant sound that was like the chirping and twittering and chattering of a thousand starlings. And, gazing down at the main highway that led out of the mountains, he saw them going past – what seemed an endless procession of princesses, with their fluttering ribbons and laces and kerchiefs, cloaks and trains and petticoats and veils a-blowing in the wind. A whole hundred of them, in twos and threes, jabbering and jostling, singing and laughing and giggling, down the rocky pass.

I'm glad I'm up here, not down there, thought Dan.

But, by and by, he heard the tramping of a horse's hoofs, and here came the young knight in his gold crown, with a princess, very young and pretty, sitting pillion on the saddle behind him. And a droopy dragon following them, at the end of a long cord.

'*It worked!*' shouted the young knight joyfully. 'It really worked! A thousand, thousand thanks! I'm everlastingly grateful to you – and so are all the princesses.'

The one riding behind him smiled down at Dan, very friendly. She didn't seem to notice the glass patches all over his skin.

'Won't you come down with us to the city?' said the young man. 'I shall be king one day, and I'll make you my prime minister.'

'No, I thank you, your worship,' said Dan. 'I'd sooner stay here. Besides, people might not respect a prime minister with glass patches all over him. But I'm much obliged for the offer. Only tell me,' he went on, full of curiosity, 'what happened?'

'Why! As soon as the dragons saw the word written in dew on my forehead they all curled up and withered away in flakes of ash. All except this one, which I'm taking to the Zoo. I'd say,' the knight told Dan, 'there wasn't a dragon left now

73

between here and the Western Ocean. Which is all due to you. So I thank you again.'

And with that he set spurs to his horse, and started off down the hill, slipping and sliding, with the dragon limping along behind, and the princess waving thanks and blowing kisses to Dan, until they were out of sight.

All the time they were in view, Dan stood gaping after them. Then he slapped his thighs. Then he began to laugh, and he laughed so hard that he fell down, and Buff stared at him in disapproval.

'It worked!' shouted Dan. 'It really worked! Dragons are bound by cords, and men by words.'

He lay laughing up at the sky, with the larks twittering overhead.

Then he thought: 'What word shall I think of next?'

He damped his finger in the morning dew and wrote on his own forehead.

A growl of thunder rumbled above him, and a lance of lightning flashed like a knitting needle out of a black ball of cloud.

'All right, all right,' shouted Dan, waving gaily to the sky. 'Just keep calm up there, will you? We won't have any of that for the moment. One word at a time is enough.'

And he sat himself down on a rock to watch his sheep.

WHO DO YOU KNOW?

Peter Dickinson

Look out of the bus window –
Hundreds of houses going by
All full of people you don't know at all.
And when they look out of their windows
Hundreds of people go by
They don't know at all.
That's hundreds of hundreds of people
All seeing hundreds more people they don't know.
Count up, and you soon get to a world
Full of people who don't know each other.
(There is a fallacy, of course.)

How many people *do* you know?
Can you get up to a hundred?
And how many people do *they* know?
Start multiplying, just the same way,
And you soon get to a world
Full of people who know someone
Who knows someone who knows someone
Who knows someone who knows someone
– It only needs five someones –
Who knows YOU.
(There is a fallacy, of course.)

TEETH

Jan Mark

Eric still lives in the town where we grew up. He says he wants to stay close to his roots. That's a good one. You can say that again. Roots.

Some people are rich because they are famous. Some people are famous just for being rich. Eric Donnelly is one of the second sort, but I knew him before he was either, when we were at Victoria Road Primary together. I don't really *know* Eric any more, but I can read about him in the papers any time, same as you can. He was in one of the colour supplements last Sunday, with a photograph of his house all over a double-page spread. You need a double-page spread to take in Eric these days. He was being interviewed about the things he really considers important in life, which include, in the following order, world peace, conservation, foreign travel (to promote world peace, of course, not for *fun*), his samoyeds (a kind of very fluffy wolf) and his wife. He didn't mention money but anyone who has ever known Eric – for three years like I did or even for five minutes – knows that on Eric's list it comes at the top, way in front of world peace. In the photo he was standing with the wife and three of the samoyeds in front of the house, trying to look ordinary. To *prove* how ordinary he is he was explaining how he used to be very poor and clawed his way up using only his own initiative. Well, that's true as far as it goes: his own initiative and his own claws – and other people's teeth. He didn't mention the teeth.

'Well,' says Eric modestly, in the Sunday supplement, 'it's a standing joke, how I got started. Cast-iron baths.' That too is true as far as it goes. When Eric was fifteen he got a job with one of those firms that specialize in house clearances. One day they cleared a warehouse which happened to contain two hundred and fifty Victorian cast-iron baths with claw feet. It occurred to Eric that there were a lot of people daft enough to actually *want* a Victorian bath with claw feet; people, that is, who hadn't had to grow up with them, so he bought the lot at a knock-down price, did them up and flogged them. That bit's well known, but in the Sunday supplement he decided to come clean. He came clean about how he'd saved enough money to buy the baths in the first place by collecting scrap metal, cast-offs, old furniture and returnable bottles. 'A kind of rag-and-bone man,' said Eric, with the confidence of a tycoon who can afford to admit that he used to be a rag-and-bone man because he isn't one any more. He still didn't mention the teeth.

I first met Eric Donnelly in the Odeon one Saturday morning during the kids' show. I'd seen him around at school before – he was in the year above mine – but here he was sitting next to me. I was trying to work out one of my front teeth which had been loose for ages and was now hanging by a thread. I could open and shut it, like a door, but it kept getting stuck and I'd panic in case it wouldn't go right side round again. In the middle of the millionth episode of *Thunder Riders* it finally came unstuck and shot out. I just managed to field it and after having a quick look I shoved it in my pocket. Eric leaned over and said in my earhole, 'What are you going to do with that, then?'

'Put it under me pillow,' I said. 'Me mum'll give me sixpence for it.'

'Oh, the tooth fairy,' said Eric. I hadn't quite liked to mention the tooth fairy. I was only eight but I knew already what happened to lads who went round talking about fairies.

'Give it to us, then,' Eric said. 'I'll pay you sixpence.'

'Do you collect them?' I asked him.

77

'Sort of,' said Eric. 'Go on – sixpence. What about it?'

'But me mum knows it's loose,' I said.

'Sevenpence, then.'

'She'll want to know where it went.'

'Tell her you swallowed it,' Eric said. 'She won't care.'

He was right, and I didn't care either, although I cared a lot about the extra penny. You might not believe this, but a penny – an old penny – was worth something then, that is, you noticed the difference between having it and not having it. I've seen my own kids lose a pound and not think about it as much as I thought about that extra penny. Eric was already holding it out on his palm in the flickering darkness – one penny and two threepenny bits. I took them and gave him the tooth in a hurry – I didn't want to miss any more of *Thunder Riders*.

'Your tooth's gone, then,' my mum said, when I came home and she saw the gap.

'I swallowed it,' I said, looking sad. 'Never mind,' she said, and I could see she was relieved that the tooth fairy hadn't got to fork out another sixpence. I'd lost two teeth the week before. They started coming out late but once they got going there was no holding them and my big brother Ted was still shedding the odd grinder. She gave me a penny, as a sort of consolation prize, so I was tuppence up on that tooth. I didn't tell her about flogging it to Eric Donnelly for sevenpence. She'd have thought it was a bit odd. I thought it was a bit odd myself.

It was half-term that weekend so I didn't see Eric till we were back at school on Wednesday. Yes, Wednesday. Half-terms were short, then, like everything else: trousers, money . . . He was round the back of the bog with Brian Ferris.

'Listen,' Eric was saying, 'threepence, then.'

'Nah,' said Brian, 'I want to keep it.'

'But you said your mum didn't believe in the tooth fairy,' Eric persisted. 'You been losing teeth for two years for *nothing*! If you let me have it you'll get threepence – *four*pence.'

'I want it,' said Brian. 'I want to keep it in a box and watch it go rotten.'

'Fivepence,' said Eric.

'It's mine. I want it.' Brian walked away and Eric retired defeated, but at dinner time I caught him at it again with Mary Arnold, over by the railings.

'How much does your tooth fairy give you?' he asked.

'A shilling,' said Mary, smugly.

'No deal, then,' Eric said, shrugging.

'But I'll let *you* have it for thixpenth,' said Mary, and smiled coyly. She always was soft, that Mary.

I started to keep an eye on Eric after that, him and his collection. It wasn't *what* he was collecting that was strange – Tony Mulholland collected bottle tops – it was the fact that he was prepared to pay. I noticed several things. First, the size of the tooth had nothing to do with the amount that Eric would cough up. A socking great molar might go for a penny, while a little worn-down bottom incisor would change hands at sixpence or sevenpence. Also, that he would never go above elevenpence. That was his ceiling. No one ever got a shilling out of Eric Donnelly, even for a great big thing with roots. Charlie McEvoy had one pulled by the dentist and brought it to school for Eric but Eric only gave him sevenpence for it.

'Here, Charlie,' I said, at break. 'What's he do with them?'

'Search me,' said Charlie, 'he's had three of mine.'

'D'you have a tooth fairy at home?' I was beginning to smell a rat.

'Yes,' said Charlie. 'Let's go and beat up Ferris.' He was a hard man, was McEvoy; started early. He's doing ten years for GBH right now, and the Mulhollands are waiting for him when he comes out.

'No – hang about. How much?'

'Sixpence.' I was quite surprised. I wouldn't have put it past old McEvoy to keep a blunt instrument under the pillow, bean the tooth fairy and swipe the night's takings. He was a big fellow, even at eight. I wasn't quite so big, but Eric, although he was a year older, was smaller than me. That day I followed him home.

It was not easy to follow Eric home. They tended to marry early in that family so Eric not only had a full set of grandparents but also two great-grandmothers and enough aunties to upset the national average. As his mum seemed to have a baby about every six months Eric was always going to stay with one of them or another. He was heading for one of his great-grandmas that evening, along Jubilee Crescent. I nailed him down by the phone box.

'Listen, Donnelly,' I said. 'What are you doing with all them teeth?'

Give him credit, he didn't turn a hair. A lot of kids would have got scared, but not Eric. He just said, 'You got one for me, then?'

'Well, no,' I said, 'but I might have by Saturday.'

'Sevenpence?' said Eric, remembering the previous transaction, I suppose. He had a head for figures.

'Maybe,' I said, 'but I want to know what you do with them.'

'What if I won't tell you?' Eric said.

'I'll knock all yours out,' I suggested, so he told me. As I thought, it was all down to the grannies and aunties. They were sorry for poor little Eric – Dad out of work, all those brothers and sisters and no pocket money. If he lost a tooth while he was staying with one of them he put it under the pillow and the tooth fairy paid up. There being two great-grannies, two grannies and seven aunties, it was hard for anyone to keep tabs on the number of teeth Eric lost and it hadn't taken him long to work out that if he didn't overdo things he could keep his eleven tooth fairies in business for years. Kids who didn't have a tooth fairy of their own were happy to flog him a fang for a penny. If he had to pay more than sixpence the tooth went to Great-Granny Ennis, who had more potatoes than the rest of them put together.

By the time that he was eleven I calculate that Eric Donnelly had lost one hundred teeth, which is approximately twice as many as most of us manage to lose in a lifetime. With the money he saved he bought a second-hand barrow and toured the streets touting for scrap, returnable bottles and so on, which was what earned him enough to buy the two hundred and fifty Victorian baths with claw feet which is the beginning of the public part of Eric's success story, where we came in. I suppose there is some justice in the fact that at thirty-eight Eric no longer has a single tooth he can call his own.

No – I am not Eric's dentist. I am his dustman, and I sometimes catch a glimpse of the old cushion grips as I empty the bin. Occasionally I turn up just as Eric is leaving for a board meeting. He flashes his dentures at me in a nervous grin and I give him a cheery wave like honest dustmen are meant to do.

'Morning, Donnelly,' I shout merrily. 'Bought any good teeth lately?' He hates that.

ANOTHER BRANDRETHISM

The total number of different combinations of the 26 letters of the alphabet is 403291461126605635584000000. In a thousand million years the entire population of the world couldn't write out all the combinations, supposing that they each wrote twenty pages a day and each page contained twenty different combinations of letters.

Amazing, isn't it?

GYLES BRANDRETH

PATHS

John Christopher

Having decided to take the long way home through the fields, he found it easy to talk himself into the still longer route through the wood. When he had been little he had thought wild animals lived in it: wolves and bears. Later he heard tales of its being haunted. He didn't believe them, but even at eleven he could frighten himself at night by imagining being taken somehow from his bed and finding himself alone there. A summer afternoon was different, though.

Before entering the wood, he looked back. The new junior school from which he had just come lay in bright sunlight; it glittered especially from the solar panels on the south side of the tower. The panels extended outwards from the top, giving it a weird shape. The tower looked a bit like a bird with half-folded wings, getting ready to fly.

Trees crowded close. Usually there was birdsong, but today it was very quiet. All he heard were his footsteps on the soft earth, the occasional crackle of a twig. He came to the place, roughly at the wood's centre, where there was a grassy mound, three or four metres across. The path skirted the mound, and normally the clearing would have been sunlit; surprisingly, the tree tops were lost in a mist. Two more things surprised him. Other paths he had never seen led into the clearing; and there was a girl sitting on the mound.

She wore funny clothes, and a lot of them: a white dress, white stockings, laced-up white boots. The dress was buttoned to the neck, with long sleeves and starched cuffs, and reached nearly to her ankles. She had long dark hair under a straw hat with blue ribbons. Her face was pale, eyes brown.

Her nose was a bit long. She wouldn't have been pretty, he decided, even in normal clothes.

Going towards her, he asked: 'What's all this, then – fancy dress?'

She paused before answering. 'Who are you?' Her voice was light but sharp, and very precise. 'Are you a farmer's boy?'

She must be crackers: how could he be a farm worker, at his age?

'I'm Kevin Luscombe. I live in Southleigh. What's your name?'

She hesitated again. 'Arabella Cartwright. Where, in Southleigh?'

'Cherrytree Road.'

She shook her head. 'There's no such place. Only London Road and Dover Road, and the Green.'

She spoke like someone describing a village. Those were all streets in the old part of the town: the Green was the main shopping centre.

She was staring at him suspiciously. 'What's that, written across your jersey?'

He glanced down at his T-shirt. 'You can read, can't you?'

'It says: "The Tripods are Coming". What does it mean?'

'It's a new TV serial – science fiction. My dad knows one of the cameramen.'

She said doubtfully: 'Science fiction? Teevy? Camera men?'

He looked at her dress again, remembering something else from television – about Victorian children living near a railway line. Feeling a bit foolish, he said: 'What year is it?'

'Don't be silly!'

'Go on. Tell me. What year?'

'Eighteen eighty-four. You know that.'

'No,' he said, 'I don't. And it isn't. It's nineteen. Nineteen eighty-four.'

*

83

They sat on the mound and talked, and came to a kind of understanding. If you thought of time as a spinning wheel, with the years as spokes, this was the hub. There was no way of knowing how or why each had got here. The wood had been spoken of in her time, Arabella said, as a magic place: the mound was said to hide a ruin from ancient times.

They were curious about each other's worlds; she more so, since while he knew something about hers from history, his was totally unknown to her. He spoke of flying machines, radio and television. She said wistfully: 'I'd love to see some of it.'

He looked at her. 'Why not? Which path did you come by?' She pointed. 'That one's mine. I can take you along it, to my time.'

She said no at first – scared, he guessed. He kept on; she wavered, and eventually agreed. But as they slid off the mound, they saw someone approaching along one of the other paths.

It was a boy about their age, dressed in a tight-fitting green tunic with a padded front reaching to mid thigh. Puffed sleeves were slashed at elbow and shoulder to show a crimson shirt underneath. It looked like silk, as did the striped red and yellow stockings which covered his legs down to soft leather boots. He wore a pointed hat, with feathers at the back. He stopped when he saw them, and muttered something.

Kevin asked him: 'What year are you from?'

'Who art tha?'

It sounded part fearful, part angry. Kevin tried to explain, but he did not seem to understand.

'Who art tha?', he repeated. 'Frenchies? Spaniards, mayhap? 'Tis certain tha'rt not English.'

'Of course we're English!'

They both tried quizzing him, but did not get far. His accent

84

was thick, Irish-sounding. Suddenly he said: 'My horse.' It sounded like 'hairse'. 'She's not well tethered. I mun see to it.'

He turned and went back along the path, almost running. Kevin said: 'From what time, do you think? Elizabethan?'

'His clothes would suggest it. And when I mentioned Mary Queen of Scots, he called her "that traitress", as though she were alive still. I was reading about her lately: she was beheaded in fifteen eighty-seven.'

'So he could be from fifteen eighty-four?'

'Yes, I would think so.'

'Then what about seventeen eighty-four, or sixteen eighty-four?'

'They may still come. Or perhaps no one went into the wood in those years.'

He shrugged. 'Anyway, I was taking you to nineteen eighty-four.'

She followed silently, obviously nervous. He reached the edge of the wood and stopped to let her come up with him; then saw she had stopped, too, a couple of metres back. In a low voice, she said: 'No.'

'There's nothing to be frightened of. We don't need to go into the town. You can look at things from a distance.'

'No. I'm sorry.'

She turned back, and he followed. She was a girl, of course; he ought not to be surprised at timidness being stronger than curiosity.

When they got back to the mound, a boy was there: younger and smaller than the one in Elizabethan finery, and looking little better than a savage. He wore a smock of coarse grey cloth, roughly stitched with twine, and nothing else. His hair was tousled; arms, legs and feet thickly grimed. A bare sole of foot looked like a pad of black leather. He was playing with a pebble, and clenched it inside his fist when he saw them.

They tried questioning him, too, but with even less success. He spoke in a growling inarticulate voice. Kevin asked Arabella: 'Did you understand any of that?'

'A word, here and there. I'm sure he said "wood". Isn't that an old English word?'

'Is it?'

'He might be Saxon.'

From 984, Kevin wondered. Or 884? Wouldn't that be about the time Alfred the Great was trying to hold back the Danes?

He said: 'I don't fancy going along his path, whenever he's from.'

Arabella shivered. 'No, indeed.'

'On the other hand, I wouldn't mind taking a look into *your* time.'

She smiled. It was a nice smile; her nose wasn't really long.

'I'd like to show you.'

As he followed her, it occurred to him that they had no idea how long the wood might stay open to travellers from the different centuries. What if it closed up, and he was forced to stay in 1884? Well, he would miss his parents, sister, friends at school. On the other hand, it would certainly be exciting! And if he could remember details of one or two important inventions of the past hundred years, he might become famous, rich . . .

The shock hit him without warning as the trees thinned to show open space ahead: it brought sharp fear, a sickness in the stomach. He tried to force his way forward and managed a couple of steps, but no more. He was shivering.

Arabella turned round. 'What is it, Kevin?' She looked at him. 'You can't either, can you?'

He made an effort which brought sweat to his brow, and shook his head.

She said quietly: 'I wondered. I thought perhaps it wasn't just me. We can't get into any year except our own.'

He felt defeated and ashamed. 'I suppose we'd better go back, to the mound.'

'You must, to find your path.' Her voice was low. 'This is mine.'

'We can . . . talk.'

'We have talked.' She managed a shadowy smile. 'I'm glad we met.'

He said: 'Don't go yet!'

She came towards him, and he thought she had changed her mind. But all she did was lean forward and briefly kiss him. The straw hat was harsh against his skin, but her lips were soft.

'Goodbye, Kevin.'

In the field beyond the wood a man with a plough followed two horses. He watched her out of sight, but she didn't look back. He walked down the path, wondering what would happen to her, and corrected himself: what *had* happened. There was no way of knowing – or was there? The old churchyard at the back of the Green . . . She could have moved away from Southleigh, of course, but she might not. It wasn't likely to be Arabella Cartwright; she would probably have married. But there weren't that many Arabellas, and he knew her year of birth. 'R.I.P. Arabella —, born 1873, beloved wife of . . .' He let the thought go. He knew he wasn't going to look for that gravestone.

The clearing was empty, but he saw the savage boy on one of the paths, returning to whatever barbarous home he had come from. At least Arabella had gone back to a solid, comfortable world. Without TV or video, cars or aeroplanes or computers, but a hopeful world; good in itself and with better things to come. He and she had that in common.

He wondered about the savage boy's world. He had no temptation to go into it, even if that were possible, but it would

87

do no harm to look. There might be knights riding across the hillside, or Vikings – Roman soldiers, even.

He followed, and caught sight of him again as he reached the edge of the wood. Just as the boy stepped into the open, he dropped the pebble he had been playing with. Kevin fought the same feeling of resistance and sickness as he walked the last few metres. He picked up the pebble and called out, but the boy walked on, unhearing. He walked across an empty untilled field: no knights, Vikings, Roman soldiers. No buildings, either.

Apart from a ruin of some sort, in the distance. It was overgrown, shapeless except for one bit that stood out. Ivy trailed from a shattered tower. The outline was blurred, yet he could still recognize it. A bird with a half-folded wing, getting ready to fly . . . long broken and abandoned.

Kevin looked at the pebble he had picked up. It wasn't a pebble, in fact, but a thin square of battered metal, with a panel of crazed plastic let in one side. Behind that it was just possible to make out the face of a digital watch.

He let it drop and ran down the path, heading for home.

CAN IT BE A BRANDRETHISM?

If you could count at the rate of 200 a minute – that's going '1, 2, 3, 4, 5, 6, 7, 8, 9, 10, 11, 12' right up to '197, 198, 199, 200' in exactly 60 seconds – to count to a billion would take you 9,512 years, 342 days, 5 hours and 20 minutes.

Amazing, isn't it?

GYLES BRANDRETH

NINETY-NINE, THUMP

John Rowe Townsend

It's an old riddle: What goes ninety-nine, thump?

You know the answer, of course: A centipede with a wooden leg.

If it hadn't been for Major Delacorte-Smith, we'd have gone ninety-nine, thump in the sponsored cricket-match. I mean, we'd have been all out for ninety-nine when we needed a hundred. It was thanks to the Major and to Beryl Holroyd that we got the last run and the school got the minibus.

But I seem to have started at the end of the story. So I'll go back to the beginning. It was our games teacher, Mr Parker (called Nosy), who thought of the sponsored cricket-match. And it was his fault that it was needed, because he'd crashed the school's old minibus, and the insurance money was nothing like enough to buy a new one. We'd been having events in aid of the Minibus Fund ever since it happened. A concert, a swimming gala, a parents' dance, a Grand Fête, to say nothing of small stuff like jumble sales and coffee mornings – you name it, and if it was a way of raising money we'd had it. And with the school year nearly over, there still wasn't quite enough in the kitty. Minibuses cost a bomb.

'Just one last push is what we need,' said Jonah (that's Mr Jones, the Head) when the School Committee met, about three weeks before the end of term. The School Committee consists of three teachers and three of us pupils – Tony Keene and Christine Tranter and me – with the Head as chairman to keep an eye on us. 'I think,' Jonah went on, 'we should have a sponsored something. The question is, a sponsored *what*?'

So people suggested sponsored walks and sponsored runs

and sponsored climbs and various other things, ranging from sponsored silence to sponsored homework (which brought loud groans from those of us who would have to do it). And then Mr Parker came up with his idea of a sponsored cricket-match.

'How do you sponsor a cricket-match?' asked Jonah.

'Easy,' said Mr Parker. 'The players get people to sponsor them for every run they score, if they're batsmen, and every wicket they take, if they're bowlers. Now suppose you're a batsman and you get twelve people to sponsor you at five-pence a run, and then you score twenty runs, that's twelve pounds you've made for the Fund . . .'

'Sounds optimistic to me,' said Jonah.

'I think it's a great idea!' said Tony Keene, who fancies himself as a batsman. He was smirking all over his face. I could read his mind like a horror-comic. He was thinking there'd be lots of glory in it for *him*.

'*I* don't think it's fair,' said Christine Tranter. 'It's the boys who play cricket. Why not something for girls?'

Mr Parker pointed out that girls had won most of the prizes at the swimming gala and said it didn't matter if the boys were favoured this time. And Christine gave way, though she went on grousing a bit on principle.

'It takes two teams to play cricket,' Jonah pointed out. 'Who's going to play who?'

'*Whom*,' said Nosy, who teaches English as well as games, and corrects people's grammar automatically. Then he went on, 'Well, it has to be a school match, and it has to be a specially attractive one, so that there'll be lots of interest and we can charge for admission.' And then he added, with an air of great brilliance, 'We'll play Grangethorpe!'

'You're not serious,' said the Head. 'We never play Grangethorpe.'

Grangethorpe is the private school at the other side of town.

We don't have anything to do with it. It might as well be on Mars.

'Aha!' said Nosy. 'You know who their Head is?'

'Of course I do,' said Jonah. 'Major Delacorte-Smith. He *owns* the place.'

'In his day,' said Nosy, 'Major Delacorte-Smith was a pretty good cricketer. He captained a Minor County eleven. Now, if we could interest *him* . . .'

'Well, why don't you look into it?' said the Head. He sounded a bit bored. I don't think he expected anything to come of the idea. But Nosy did look into it. A couple of days later, he called me over to him and said, 'The match against Grangethorpe is *on*. You'd better choose your side, and then we'll get busy on the sponsorship.'

Our school doesn't have anything as posh as a games captain, but when it comes to cricket I'm usually it. I can't bat like Tony Keene, but I can bowl a bit, and I have more sense than he has.

So I chose my team and pinned the names up on the notice-board. Christine Tranter was still sour. 'Eleven boys!' she complained. 'Not a single girl. *Typical!*'

'Don't be daft,' I told her. 'Girls don't play cricket.'

'I know one who does,' she said. 'Beryl Holroyd. I've seen her bat. She's terrific!'

Beryl Holroyd was a skinny kid who's only been at our school a few months. I didn't think she was likely to be any good. But I wanted to show I wasn't biased. So I cornered her in the playground and asked about it.

'I play with me brothers,' she said. 'There's six of 'em.'

'Phew! Six brothers! Where do you come from?'

'Pudsey. In Yorkshire.'

Well, some pretty good cricketers come from Pudsey. You should hear my dad go on about Herbert Sutcliffe and Len Hutton and Ray Illingworth. 'I'll bowl to you after school,' I said. And I did. And it didn't take five minutes to convince me that Christine was right. Beryl was in the team, in place of Wally Lockwood, who wasn't all that keen to play anyway.

The sponsorship worked a treat. My family and the neighbours all backed me for various amounts. In the end every run I made was going to be worth forty-five pence towards that minibus, and every wicket I took would bring in more than a pound. Tony Keene was only backed for thirty pence a run, but he was likely to make a lot more than I did. And Beryl had done best of all. When she took her sponsorship sheet round, people laughed at her and put themselves down for all kinds of fancy sums. In the end Beryl was worth nearly two pounds for every run she made.

'Why don't you go over to Grangethorpe and see Major Delacorte-Thingummy?' asked my dad a few days before the match. 'See if *he'll* sponsor you. There's nothing like a bit of cheek.'

I wasn't too keen on that, but my dad insisted and ran me round there. And I got to see the Major without any trouble. He was a nice old guy. Thin, with greying fair hair and sharp, bright blue eyes.

'I'll sponsor your whole team,' he said at once. 'Ten pence a run for the lot of you, and double if you beat us. But I don't think you will. My boys are pretty keen. I coach them myself.'

The match was at our school. It was a fine Saturday afternoon, and lots of people paid to watch. The Grangethorpe mob turned up on time. I'd expected them to be a lot of snobs, but they were quite ordinary: pretty much like us, in fact. They batted first and made 99, which is a good score in our class of cricket. I took six wickets for 34 and earned seven pounds twenty for the fund.

Then it was our turn. Tony Keene opened and was out first ball for a duck. I didn't mind him being taken down a peg, but it was no use to the fund. After that we crawled along and had half our wickets down for 28 and two more down before we were forty. One of them was mine, clean bowled for one pound eighty; I mean, four runs. We weren't doing too well.

That was when Beryl Holroyd came in. The Grangethorpe lot were sniggering. All the fielders moved in closer. I thought for a minute their fast bowler was going to bowl underarm. He didn't actually do that, but he tossed up a high, slow ball. Wham! Straight to the legside boundary. Four runs for Beryl. Eight pounds at a stroke.

And so it went on. Six brothers and Pudsey had taught her any amount of technique, and you wouldn't believe the strength there was in those skinny wrists. Grangethorpe threw all they had against her. The fast bowler got ever faster, and more inaccurate, until he slipped and turned an ankle on his run-up, and the Major himself came on as a substitute fielder. He didn't bowl, of course. Beryl went on hitting. Mick Darling and Dan James were caught out at the other end, but the last man, Neil Perry, hung on while Beryl made the runs. Suddenly we were on 99 and the scores were tied.

Then, at last, Beryl mis-hit a good ball, high into the sky. She and Neil had taken a run before it came down – into the hands of Major Delacorte-Smith. I groaned. It looked as though we'd just failed to win, and get the double payment he'd promised us. Ninety-nine, thump. And then . . . the ball fell through the Major's hands on to the ground.

'Oh, sir! Sir! Sir!' The Grangethorpe mob were wailing re-proaches at him. They could hardly believe it. But our score was a hundred, and we'd won. And although we didn't quite make the amount needed to reach the Minibus Fund target, we were so close to it that Jonah was able to twist a few people's arms and get the rest by the end of term.

I saw the Major after the match. He'd just been congratulat-ing Beryl, and he came to ask how much he owed us. I told him. Then I said – it was cheeky, but I couldn't help it – 'I was amazed when you dropped that catch. I mean *you*, a *real* cricketer.'

'Well . . .' said the Major. There was a long pause. He looked at me and I looked at him.

'I dropped it in a good cause,' he said.

---

100 – OR MORE

Gyles Brandreth

Here is a trick to try out on your friends. To play the trick you have to make your victim think of a three-digit number. It could be anything from 100 to 999. Here's what you do:

1. Get your friend to pick any three-digit number.
2. Get them to repeat the three-digit number to form a six-digit number.
3. Divide the number by 7.
4. Divide the answer by 11.
5. Divide this answer by 13.
6. And lo and behold, believe it or not, you'll end up with the same number you started with!

It doesn't seem possible, but here's the proof:

1. Let's choose 529 as the three-digit number.
2. Now we repeat it: 529,529
3. Now we divide it by 7:   75,644
4. Now we divide 75,644 by 11:   6,874
5. Now we divide 6,874 by 13:   529!

THE FLYING KING

Terry Jones

There was once a devil in Hell whose name was Carnifex, who liked to eat small children. Sometimes he would take them alive and crush all the bones in their bodies, sometimes he would pull their heads off and sometimes he would hit them so hard that their backs snapped like dry twigs – oh! There was no end to the terrible things he could do. But one day Carnifex got out of his bed in Hell to find there was not a single child left.

'What I need is a regular supply,' he said to himself. So he went to a country that he knew was ruled by an exceedingly vain king, and found him in his bathroom (which contained over a hundred baths) and said to him: 'How would you like to fly?'

'Very much indeed,' said the king, 'but what do you want in return, Carnifex?'

'Oh . . . nothing very much,' replied Carnifex, 'and I will enable you to fly as high as you want, as fast as you want, simply by raising your arms like this,' and he showed the king how he could fly.

'I should indeed like to be able to do that,' thought the king to himself. 'But what is it you want in return, Carnifex?' he asked aloud.

'Look! Have a try!' replied Carnifex. 'Put out your arms – that's right, and now off you go!'

And the king put out his arms, and immediately he floated into the air, then he soared over the roofs and chimney-pots of the city, then he went higher and higher, until he was above the clouds, and he flew like a bird on a summer's day. Then he landed back beside the devil and said:

'But what *is* it you want in return, Carnifex?'

'Oh nothing much,' replied Carnifex, 'just give me one small child every day, and you shall be able to fly just like that.'

Now the king was indeed very anxious to be able to fly just like that, but he knew the terrible things that Carnifex did to small children, so he shook his head.

'I'm sorry,' he said, 'I would willingly give you each and every one of my own sons and daughters if I could always fly just like that, but I have only thirty of them and that would barely keep me in the air for a month.'

'But there are thousands of children in your kingdom,' replied Carnifex. 'I shall only take one a day – your people will hardly notice.'

The king thought long and hard about this, for he knew it was an evil thing, but in the end he agreed, and from that day on he could fly just like that.

To begin with all his subjects were very impressed. The first time he took to the air, a great crowd gathered in the main square and stood there open-mouthed as they watched their king spread out his arms, rise into the air, and then soar up beyond the clouds and out of sight. Then he swooped down again and flew low over their heads, while they all clapped and cheered.

But after a few months it became such a common sight to see their king flying up over the city that the people all got quite used to it. Some of them even began to resent it. And every day some poor family would find that one of their children had been taken by Carnifex, the devil.

Now it so happened that the king's youngest daughter had a favourite doll that was so lifelike that she loved it and treated it just as if it had been a real live baby. And she was in the habit of stealing into the king's bathroom, when he wasn't looking, to bath this doll in one of his baths. And it so happened that she was doing this on the very day that the king made his pact with

Carnifex, and so it was she overheard every word that passed between them.

Naturally she was terrified by what she had heard, but because girls were not reckoned much of in that country and in those days, and because she was the least and most insignificant of all his daughters, she had not dared to tell anyone what she had heard. But one day, Carnifex came and took the king's own favourite son.

The king busied himself in his counting-house and would not say a word, and later that day he went off for a long flight, and did not return until well after dark. But the boy's mother was so overcome with grief she could not speak, and she took to her bed and seemed likely to die.

Then the youngest daughter came to her, as always clutching her favourite doll, and told her all she knew. At once the queen's grief turned to anger against the king. But she was a shrewd woman, and she knew that if she went to the king and complained he would, as like as not, have her head chopped off before she could utter another word. So instead she dressed herself as a beggarwoman, and took the youngest daughter and crept out of the palace at dead of night. Then she went about the kingdom, far and wide, begging her way. And everywhere she went she got the youngest daughter to stand on a stool, still clutching her favourite doll (which everyone thought was real), and tell her story. And everywhere they went everyone who heard the tale said: 'So *that's* how the king can fly.' And everywhere everyone was filled with anger against the king.

Eventually all the people from all the corners of the realm came to the king to protest. They gathered in the main square, and the king hovered above them looking distinctly uneasy.

'You are not worthy to be our king!' the people cried. 'You have sacrificed our very children just so that you can fly!'

The king fluttered up a little higher, so he was just out of reach, and then he ordered them all to be quiet, and called out: 'Carnifex! Where are you?'

There was a flash and a singeing smell, and Carnifex the devil appeared sitting on top of the fountain in the middle of the square.

At once a great cry went up from the crowd – something between fear and anger – but Carnifex shouted: 'Listen! I understand how you feel!'

The people were rather taken aback by these words, and one or two of them even began to think that perhaps Carnifex wasn't such a bad fellow after all, and some of the ladies began to notice he was quite handsome – in his devilish sort of way . . . But the king's youngest daughter stood up on her stool, and cried out: 'He's a devil! Don't listen to him!'

'Quite quite,' said Carnifex, licking his lips at the sight of the little girl still clutching her favourite doll. 'But even I can sympathize with the tragic plight of parents who see their own beloved offspring snatched away in front of their very eyes.'

'Well fancy that!' said more than one citizen to his neighbour.

'Whoever would have thought he would be such a gentleman . . .' whispered more than one housewife to her best friend.

'Don't listen!' shouted the king's youngest daughter.

'So I'll tell you what I'll do,' said Carnifex, never taking his beady eyes off the little girl clutching what he thought was a small baby, 'I'll give you some compensation for your tragic losses. I will let you all fly – just like that!' – and he pointed at the king, who flew up and down a bit and then looped the loop just to show them all what it was like. And there was not a single one of those good people who wasn't filled with an almost unbearable desire to join him in the air.

'Don't listen to him!' shouted the little girl. 'He'll want your children!'

'All I ask,' said Carnifex in his most wheedling voice, 'is for one tiny . . . weeny . . . little child a day. Surely that's not much to ask?'

And, you know, perhaps there were one or two there who were so besotted with the desire to fly that they might have agreed, had not a remarkable thing happened. The king's youngest daughter suddenly stood up on tiptoe, and held up her favourite doll so that all the crowd could see, and she cried out: 'Look! This is what he'll do to your children!' and with that she hurled the doll, which she loved so dearly, right into Carnifex's lap.

Well, of course, this was too much for the devil. He thought it was a real live baby, and he had its head off and all its limbs in pieces before you could say 'Rabbits!'

And when the crowd saw Carnifex apparently tearing a small baby to pieces (for none of them knew it was just a doll) they came to their senses at once. They gave an angry cry, and converged on Carnifex where he crouched, with his face all screwed up in disgust, spitting out bits of china doll and stuffing.

And I don't know what they would have done if they'd laid hold of him, but before they could, he had leapt from the fountain right on to the back of the flying king, and with a cry of rage and disappointment he rode him down to Hell where they both belonged.

And after that, the people gave the youngest daughter a new doll that was just as lifelike as the previous one, and she was allowed to bath it in the king's bathroom any day she wanted.

As for Carnifex, he returned every year to try and induce the people to give up just one child a day to him. But no matter what he offered them they never forgot what they had seen him do that day, and so they refused, and he returned to Hell empty-handed. And all this happened hundreds and hundreds of years ago, and Carnifex never did think of anything that could persuade them.

But listen! You may think that Carnifex was a terrible devil, and you may think that the flying king was a terrible man for giving those poor children to Carnifex just so that he could fly. But I shall tell you something even more astonishing, and that is that in this very day, in this very land where you and I live, we allow not one . . . not two . . . not three . . . but *twenty* children to have their heads smashed, or their backs broken, or to be crushed alive every day – and not so that we can even fly, but just so that we can ride about in things we call motor cars. If I'd read that in a fairy tale, I wouldn't have believed it – would you?

100, 99, 98, ZZZZzzzz

Gyles Brandreth

ANOTHER BRANDRETHIZZZZMMMM

Do you ever find it difficult to get to sleep at night? If you do, instead of counting sheep, try counting numbers. If you want a challenge, try counting from 100 to 0 backwards. Every time you make a mistake, puttting 54 after 53 instead of before, you must go back to 100. The chances are you'll be fast asleep before you reach 9, 8, 7, 6, 5, 4, 3, 2, 1, 0.

UP TO 100
Gyles Brandreth

Here's an unusual game for just two players. It's called 'Up to 100'. It's simple to learn and exciting to play.

If you play the game with a friend, get him or her to start. He or she has to begin by writing down any number from 1 to 10 on a piece of paper. You then write down a second number – again it can be any number from 1 to 10 – and add the two together. He or she then writes down a third number, again any number from 1 to 10, and adds this number to the first two. You go on doing this, taking it in turns to add a number to the total. The player who adds the final number that makes the total add up to exactly 100 is the winner.

And if you like winning, you'll be pleased to know that you can win this game every time! All you have to do to win is this:

Make sure that at the end of one of your moves the total is either 12 or 23 or 34 or 45 or 56 or 67 or 78 or 89. Once you have reached one of these numbers your worries are over, because all you have to do then is play numbers which, when added to your opponent's last number, make eleven. Once you reach 89 it doesn't matter what number he calls, you can always add whatever it takes to hit 100.

It sounds complicated, but once you've worked the system a few times you will find it easy to remember. Aim for 12, 23, 34, 45, 56, 67, 78 and 89 and all will be well. And if you feel that they aren't easy numbers to remember, think of them as
> one two
>> two three
>>> three four
>>>> four five
>>>>> five six
>>>>>> six seven
>>>>>>> seven eight
>>>>>>>> eight nine
>>>>>>>>> and you're certain not to forget them.

THE HUNDREDTH FEATHER

Rosemary Sutcliff

Andros the maker of picture-floors took a cube of greenish-blue slate from the ordered scatter of tesserae beside him, and leaning forward, fitted it carefully into the place waiting for it, settling it down into the cement bedding with a few taps of his round-headed wooden mallet, and sat back on his heels. The peacock's breast was finished.

The whole floor was nearly finished. It had been early winter when he started on it, laying the key-pattern borders that made a frame for the goddess Juno and her peacock. Now it was spring. The leaves were breaking on the carefully tended rose bushes of the courtyard garden, and the jackdaws were nesting in the old army signal tower further up the hill. He

could hear their 'ka-ark' and jabber in the quiets between the gusts of March wind. In a few more days he would be on his travels again, looking for somebody else who wanted a picture-floor but could not or would not pay for a really good one.

When he was young and learning his trade, Andros had dreamed of becoming the kind of artist-craftsman that the greatest and richest people sent for from Gaul, even from Rome itself, when they wanted their floors made beautiful with pictures of the four seasons or Bacchus the wine-god in a chariot drawn by panthers. But now his hair was grey and his shoulders humped from years of stooping over his work, and he was resigned to the fact that he was a good craftsman and nothing more, and that it was only moderately prosperous merchants like Cornelius Kaeso, or the town councils of small back-woods settlements, who would not know a good pavement if they saw one, who would employ him. At least he was almost resigned. Never quite.

He shifted back a little, for a better view of the whole

pavement spread before him. The colouring was pleasant; but it could hardly be anything else, when the tesserae with which the picture was made, none of them bigger than the tip of his forefinger, were blue slate and creamy chalk, golden sandstone and soft rust-red tile. The borders were well enough; but Juno, standing with one outstretched hand on the peacock's neck, her tunic falling in elaborate folds about her, looked stiff and lumpish. His people always looked stiff and lumpish. With birds and animals he was better. He turned his attention to the peacock.

The sun, which the moment before had been behind a cloud, came out and flooded the softly coloured pavement with light; and it seemed to Andros that the peacock was beautiful. The small snake-like crested head on its slender neck turned towards its mistress, the wings drooping, half spread, and behind, the proudly arched splendour of the great fanned-out tail. One hundred feathers, from the smallest and shortest close in to its body, to the tall ox-eyed plumes of the outer rim.

There were still unfinished patches in the tail, but the position of each 'eye' was already marked, with a space left in its centre for the cube of blue glass that would catch the light of sun and lamps and moon and bring the whole to life.

The slave who had broken the big blue glass jug had been soundly whipped for it, for it was a household treasure. But Andros could not help rejoicing in the accident, and in three days of careful chipping and rubbing down he had managed to get just one hundred pieces of the right size and shape. He felt that the gods had been kind to him, if not to the slave, and he gave thanks accordingly.

A shadow fell across the patch of sunlight from the doorway, a rather small shadow, and looking up, he saw Serenilla, the daughter of the house. Serenilla was nearly eleven years old, and dull-looking and lumpish as the goddess on the pavement. But Andros, cocking a half-friendly eyebrow at her as he took up a cube of yellow sandstone – for he was used to her visits – wondered suddenly what was inside the dull

lumpishness, looking out. He was the first person who had ever wondered that.

After the windy sun-dazzle in the courtyard, it seemed dark in the new dining-room, and Serenilla stood blinking until the red and green patches faded and she could see properly again. The little grey-haired, sour-looking man squatting among the tools of his trade looked as he always did, as though he had squatted there, nothing changing, since her last visit.

But today something was changed; something to do with the peacock. There was a new life, a new magic about it. She moved, and the sunlight lancing in past her woke a flake of blue fire in the eye of one of the proud tail feathers, and another, and then another.

'Oh!' She gave a little gasp, delight waking in her. 'You've put the blue eyes into some of the peacock feathers!'

Some of the sourness went out of the man's face. 'A few, little mistress. The others are not ready yet.'

Serenilla came in, walking with care round the sides of the new pavement, and squatted down beside him.

Andros went on quietly with his task. Generally speaking he did not like people watching while he worked, but he did not mind Serenilla.

'It's nearly finished,' she said. 'It's all nearly finished' – half with a kind of contentment, and half with regret, because when it was finished, the making would be over, and she had loved the making, watching it grow under Andros's hands. She wished she could make something like that, something beautiful.

For a while she sat and watched, not speaking, not even wanting to speak . . . He took one of the precious cubes of blue glass from the crock in which they were stored, and set to placing it in the eye of one of the tallest feathers. She leaned forward to watch more closely, and the necklace she was wearing swung forward. It was just a string of cheap glass

SHIRLEY HUGHES

beads that she had bought with her own sweetmeat money from a travelling seller of such things. Her nurse said it was vulgar, and her mother had sighed when first she saw it. Neither of them liked her wearing it, though nobody had actually forbidden her. 'It's just a new toy. She'll grow tired of it soon,' she had heard her mother say, hopefully. But Serenilla knew that she would not grow tired of it, because of the blue bead. One bright and lovely bead the colour of all the clear skies of all the fine summer days since the world began. A colour that sang like a lark among all the white and brown and dull red earth-bound beads of the rest of the necklace. Almost the colour of the peacock eye that was catching the light under Andros's hand. She put up her own hand, lovingly, to touch it as it swung; and Andros said without looking round, 'You have another eye there to shine back at the sun, or the moon, or the lamps at evening.'

Serenilla reached out to touch in the same caressing way the newly set cube of glass. 'Is it the most beautiful thing you have ever made?'

He considered. It was not a question to be answered lightly. 'I think so,' he said at last.

'I think so, too,' said Serenilla, gravely.

He laughed, a little harshly. 'You have not seen anything else that I have made.'

'But I can see the peacock,' said Serenilla.

A short while later, her nurse came calling for her. 'Your mother wants you. It is time for you to try on your new tunic. Quick now!'

And Serenilla sighed, and got up, and went obediently after her across the courtyard, with a sinking heart. She knew what a disappointment she was to her mother, who so wanted a pretty daughter to dress in pretty clothes. She was a disappointment to her father, too, but it did not so much matter to

Father because there were the two boys, and he really only cared about sons, anyway. She wished he would notice her, and take her seriously, as he did the boys. She wished the boys did not treat her as a baby. She wished, oh how she wished, that Mother would not make her wear pink . . .

The jackdaw flapping over on his way back to his nest in the old signal tower gave a mocking 'ka-ark!' that sounded as though even he were laughing at the idea of Serenilla dressed in pink. She cast a glance of protest after him as she reached the opposite colonnade and the doorway to her mother's room.

'She's still such a baby. I suppose it's foolish to expect her to take any interest in her appearance, but one must try –' she heard her mother saying to a visiting woman friend, as she came in.

Soon afterwards, another shadow darkened the dining-room doorway. A much larger shadow than Serenilla's; and when Andros looked up, it was to see Cornelius Kaeso, the master of the house.

'Hrmph,' said Cornelius Kaeso, coming in with his fine stomach well in advance of the rest of him, to get a closer view of the work. 'Hrmph.'

He always said that, every time he came. Andros guessed that he did not know what else to say. Probably he would have been more at home with just the straight plait-work and key-pattern borders carving the floor up into nice manageable squares and triangles; but he had to have Juno and her peacock to show his fellow merchants that he lived in grander style than they did.

'Well, you're charging me enough for it, but I will admit that it looks worth it,' he said at last. 'Very expensive looking. Especially by lamplight.'

Andros set another cube of sandstone in place and said nothing.

'How long will you take to finish it?' Cornelius asked.

'Four days. Maybe five – and another three for the last part of it to be hard enough for use.'

'Hrmph,' said Cornelius Kaeso. 'Then I shall give a dinner – just a small dinner to a few friends – in eight days' time. Very pretty, those bits of blue glass – good idea. Yes, well, eight days' time. Be sure it's ready.' And he padded out.

Andros stared down at the peacock. It looked clumsy, lacking in all pride. 'Maybe it would look even more expensive in the dark,' he said under his breath.

The days passed. The first pair of jackdaws had almost finished their nest in the old signal tower; the garden slave had spring-pruned the roses, and the kitchen was buzzing with preparations for Cornelius Kaeso's dinner party.

The fifth day came, and Andros was putting the final touches to the peacock's tail. It was then he discovered that where the last five cubes of blue glass should have been at the bottom of the crock – there had been five yesterday, he had counted them – there were only four.

Serenilla, arriving on one of her visits, found him hunting through the folds of sacking that protected the floor where he was working. 'What is it? Have you lost something?'

Andros shook his head like a baffled bear. 'There are only four of the glass tesserae left. There should be five.'

'O-oh!' Serenilla came and sat on her heels beside him, and began to search too, looking carefully in all the places where he had just looked, so that he wanted to shout at her to leave be. But he knew that in its different way, and for some unknown reason, her caring was as deep as his own, and he did not.

'There isn't another blue glass pot anywhere in the house,' she said at last in a small hopeless voice, when they had looked everywhere.

'And if there was, I could scarcely expect Marcipar to break it

110

for me and get another flogging,' Andros said. 'And with your father's dinner party in only three days' time . . .'

'What will you do?'

'There's only one thing I *can* do – replace the eye of one of the lesser feathers with slate, and move that cube up to the top, where it shows more.'

'But if you do that, it won't be perfect.'

'It won't be perfect anyway,' Andros said savagely. 'Your father said it would look expensive by lamplight. But that's a different matter.'

Serenilla said, 'It won't have its magic, not without its whole hundred peacock-eyes to shine.' The peacock that was so nearly perfect, and yet would always now be flawed, blurred on her sight, and for a moment she was on the edge of tears. And then suddenly she knew what she must do; and knowing, she scrambled to her feet and ran.

She ran to her own little sleeping cubicle, and opened the clothes chest at the foot of the narrow bed, and rummaged inside for the painted olive-wood box in which she kept her treasures. Inside she found her silver scissors among all the tangle of other things there. Then she took off her necklace, and without giving herself time to think, cut the thread.

The beads ran pattering down into the box, all save the blue glass one, which she caught as it came off the string. She could gather them up and re-string them later. But she knew that she would not. They would not be worth re-stringing, just the white and brown and rusty-red. Still, she had no regrets. She got up without even waiting to shut the lid of her clothes chest, and ran back the way she had come.

Andros, who was delicately prising out the glass cube from the smallest and least noticeable feather, glanced round as she squatted down beside him. And something he saw in her face caught at his breath. 'Little mistress – you have not found it somewhere?'

She shook her head, and holding out her closed hand to him, opened it slowly and carefully, and he saw that lying in the cushiony hollow of her palm was the precious blue glass bead.

'It is very nearly the same colour,' she said.

They sat and looked at it together. The light striking through it made a tiny stain of living blue on Serenilla's hand where she held it; and Andros thought suddenly that it was the most beautiful thing he had ever seen.

'It is the blue bead from your necklace.'

'Yes. It's for you – for the peacock.' All at once she was afraid that he was going to treat her like a baby and say that he could not take her pretty toy.

But Andros understood how great a thing she offered, and he accepted it gravely. 'My thanks to you, for the gift. It must go here at the crowning-point, in the eye of the master feather.'

'But you have one there already.'

'No matter; I can get it out and set it elsewhere. If I put yours into a lesser feather it will throw the whole balance out, because it is more beautiful than the others, and being round, the light strikes on it differently.'

And he set to work to lift out the blue tessera that he had set into the master feather yesterday, and put it aside while he replaced it with Serenilla's blue bead. When it was done, they sat back, side by side, and looked at it.

The morning sunlight through the high window fell across the peacock, and the branches of the poplar tree outside, swaying in the spring wind, made the light flicker and dance as though the pictured bird were on the edge of life, and the points of blue fire in its tail feathers woke and darkened and woke again.

112

Andros, who had come near to hating it, saw it proud and beautiful again because someone whose sight he trusted had found enough of pride and beauty in it to make it worthy of her most treasured possession. And Serenilla knew that whenever she looked at the peacock on Father's new dining-room floor, she would know that she had had a share in making something beautiful, and she would know also that she was a real person who mattered in her own right, because the little grey man who had made the rest of the beauty had treated her that way.

The sunlight stilled for a moment, and the eye of the master feather, the hundredth feather, shone out clear and steady; a blue star.

Next day Andros moved on in search of more picture-pavements to make, and two days after that Cornelius Kaeso held his dinner party, and the lamplight woke wavering blue sparks in the new floor, which his fellow merchants politely admired, missing all the magic in it. And when the dinner was over and the lamps put out and the dining-room was empty, the moon came in through the high window and, making its own cool patterns on the pavement, struck a sharp blue point of radiance from the eye of the peacock's master feather.

And the lost hundredth cube of glass? The same moonlight, slanting in through the gap where a stone had fallen from the wall of the forsaken signal tower, was answered by a tiny point of blue light that might have been a glow-worm among the dark stick-tangle of a thieving jackdaw's nest.

ONE HUNDRED LITTLE SQUIRTS

Forrest Wilson

Edith Bolton the children's author first saw the Irish genie as her train sped across London. He sat cross-legged, and with his arms folded, on a flying carpet which kept pace with the train – and he grinned at her.

He was small and young – not more than a teenager – and he wore a green cap, a green suit and green boots. He blew a bubble out of the green bubble-gum he was chewing, then he waved to her and lifted his cap in salute.

'Huh?' Edith gasped, glancing round to see if anyone else saw him. But the compartment was empty just then. 'A leprechaun?' She blinked.

He suddenly disappeared from outside the train and re-appeared inside it, still on the carpet which floated in mid-air in front of her.

'The top o' the morning to ye, begorrah, to be sure!' he said. 'And I'm not a leprechaun, I'm a genie. Leprechauns don't have magic carpets.' He frowned, thinking. 'At least – I don't think they have! No, no, they don't.'

'A genie? An *Irish* genie?' Edith said. 'But you look like a *leprechaun*!'

'We-ell, to tell ye the truth, I'm a bit o' both. Me ould Da's a leprechaun, but me Mammy's a genie – called Jeannie!' He laughed uproariously.

'I've never heard of an Irish genie before,' Edith admitted. 'But then – who has?'

'Me name's Sweeney O'Flynn. I'm Sweeney, the genie. Or O'Flynn, the djinn, if you like.' He blew another bubble, which exploded with a loud pop.

But an Irish genie in her train, Edith reflected, was only the latest in a series of shocks she had had that morning.

To begin with, she'd received a letter from her book publisher saying that her new book was too short, and asking her to write an extra story for it – right away. But it would take her weeks to get an *idea*, never mind *write* the story, and he wanted it – complete – within days.

Then, as she put her notes for her talk and her latest paperback book into her handbag, her son Steve said:

'You're not going to Rufftown Street School to speak, are you, Mum? Wow! You'd need to've been in the SAS before you'd go anywhere near there!'

'Don't talk nonsense, Steve.'

'But haven't you heard about it? Crumbs! They say it's the wildest school in the country!'

He then related, in gory detail, just how wild it was.

His mother, naturally, didn't believe him. Mothers seldom believe what their children tell them. Boys do exaggerate, after all. The Rufftown Street pupils couldn't be *that* bad. She was confident that she could handle them, having, as a children's author, given lots of talks to schoolchildren before. And besides, their teachers would be there, wouldn't they?

Then, in the train, she had opened her handbag to touch up her lipstick, and spotted the green perfume-bottle which Steve had bought from a local antique shop for her birthday.

'If you press this bulb on it,' he had pointed out, 'the perfume sprays out. I s'pose they used these before aerosols were invented, huh, Mum?'

She lifted it out and was surprised to see that apart from '100', in spidery handwriting, there was nothing else on the label. There was no maker's name and nothing to indicate what the actual perfume was. 'What if the scent doesn't suit me?' she thought. 'And what does that "100" mean?'

115

But the Irish genie's sudden appearance had put all these thoughts out of her mind.

Not that he stayed long. For the train soon reached Rufftown Street station, Edith got out and Sweeney disappeared into thin air again.

However, all thoughts of a new story, a perfume spray-bottle and an Irish genie were forgotten when Edith saw Rufftown Street school. For a running battle between two rival gangs was taking place in the playground. Dozens of pupils fought, while one side's supporters chanted, 'Cobb's mob!' and the others yelled for 'Ruff's toughs!'

Edith picked her way through the mounds of crisp packets, sweet papers, broken bottles and crumpled coke cans which littered the playground and past the bicycle sheds which were littered with the remains of broken, vandalized bikes. She saw the gang slogans and graffiti daubed on every wall, which proclaimed: THE HEAD IS A HEAD . . . CASE! MISS YUILL IS A FOOL . . . COBB'S A YOB! RUFFIAN RULES – OK? – and so on.

She shuddered as she tried to squeeze past the fighting, feuding bodies to enter the main door. What had she let herself in for? Maybe Steve had been right after all? She decided to listen to what he told her in future!

Inside, the Head Teacher passed her on to Miss Yuill, who explained:

'We've put them into the gymnasium. There's no other room big enough. Oh, and you don't mind taking an extra class, do you?'

'Oh . . . but . . . well, you did say there would be about seventy pupils,' Edith stammered. 'Wasn't it just two classes?'

'That's right, mine and Mrs Porter's. But I'm sure you won't mind taking poor Miss Scott's thirty kids as well, will you? It's *her* turn, this week, to have a nervous breakdow . . . er, that is . . . she's off sick . . . !'

'That's one hundred children!' Edith gasped.

But before she could protest she found herself being ushered along a corridor and into the gymnasium, where she *heard* the audience before she saw it! She was pointed in the direction of the platform at the far end of the room – and promptly left on her own!

'Just talk to them till lunchtime,' yelled Miss Yuill from the door, as she and Mrs Porter, who couldn't escape quickly enough, positively ran from the room. 'But you'll get a break at ten-thirty.'

Edith reckoned she'd never be able to make herself heard above the deafening noise of the hundred screaming, shouting, swearing, fighting, transistor-radio-playing kids. And if they made all this racket and behaved like this when their teachers were present – they'd be a lot worse when the teachers had gone! She groaned.

The chairs had been set out neatly in rows, but already most of them had been kicked over – or were being used as weapons by the warring factions!

'Now children,' she began. She took her latest paperback from her handbag and tried to ignore World War Three, which was raging all round her, 'I'm here to talk about the books I write . . .'

A girl in a yellow baseball cap, sitting in the front row, interrupted her. Doris – as her T-shirt indicated – yelled at the girl next to her: 'Hey, Bimbo – where's Ruffian? He ain't 'ere.'

'Dunno. 'E'll be bunkin' off somewhere, likely.'

Bimbo wore heavy make-up, with lipstick inexpertly splattered all over her mouth and eye-liner smeared all over both cheeks.

Edith looked over at the battling boys. So Ruffian wasn't among them? Well, that was something. According to the graffiti on the school walls he was one of the gang-leaders and if he were here things could be worse!

The members of the audience who weren't fighting were

117

now climbing up, or swinging on, the ropes which hung from the ceiling. Another group climbed the wall-bars and scrambled over the pieces of gymnastic equipment, while others had unearthed the sports gear and were playing various ball-games. Edith ducked as a tennis ball whizzed past her head, consoling herself with the thought that it could have been worse – it could have been a cricket ball!

The door opened and Edith looked up, hopefully. Maybe one of the teachers, or the Head – or anyone! – was coming to rescue her? 'Oh no . . . !' she gasped.

The boy with the spiky, orange-tinted hair who clumped his way across the gymnasium in his huge steel-toe-capped bovver boots wore chains and zips all over his jeans and denim jacket. And the words in brass studs on the front of the jacket identified him: RUFFIAN RULES RUFFTOWN.

The shouting, swearing, fighting pupils stopped shouting, swearing and fighting to yell: 'Hi, Ruffian!' – like subjects greeting their king.

Edith groaned again. Things could only get worse from now on!

Ruffian clumped his bovver-booted way through his admiring throng, up to the platform. 'Wot's goin' on 'ere?' he demanded pugnaciously, his face screwing itself up until it resembled a pug-dog's. 'Who're you?'

'I – I'm here . . .' she stuttered nervously, 'to t-talk to y-you about my b-books . . .' She held her paperback out to show him.

Ruffian grabbed the book, glanced briefly at it and tossed it over his shoulder. 'Huh! Rubbish!' he snorted.

The boys who were fighting stopped: to play football – with Edith's book! Five minutes later it was a tattered mess.

Suddenly – Sweeney the genie reappeared. 'Use yer bottle, Missis!' he yelled from the side of the stage, where he floated in mid-air.

No one else seemed to notice him and while Edith was wondering if only *she* could see him the school buzzer sounded, signalling morning break-time.

The hundred horrors, led by Ruffian, shot out through the gymnasium doors like a hundred Exocet missiles homing in on a target. Edith prayed that they'd stay away and play truant for the rest of the morning!

As she sighed with relief and followed them into the corridor she asked Sweeney, who was floating alongside her: 'What do you mean, "bottle"?'

She didn't know what this slang expression meant. But before Sweeney could reply she saw Miss Yuill approaching – and Edith had a bone to pick with her!

'You left me alone with those monsters!' she raged. 'And they're running riot. Do you know that? Does the Head know? Do the police know . . . ?'

Miss Yuill guided her into the staffroom, where Edith calmed down and accepted a hot, sweet cup of tea to steady her nerves.

'You see,' Miss Yuill explained, 'it was a chance for *us* to get a break, away from them. Even for a little while. We don't often get the chance. We've got the little squirts all day, every day, all week, all term – for ever . . . ! You've only got them for one morning!'

Edith suddenly remembered. 'My handbag! I left it in there. Supposing those little horrors . . . ?'

She threw down her empty cup and ran from the room. She flung open the gymnasium doors and there, near the platform, were Doris and Bimbo going through the contents of her bag.

'Leave that alone!' she yelled as she ran to the stage and grabbed her purse, which Doris had lifted out and was about to open!

Bimbo found the old-fashioned perfume spray-bottle. 'Hey,

119

wot's this, Miss? Eh?' She pointed at the label. 'An' wot does "100" mean?'

'Don't touch it!'

This, of course, was the wrong thing to say to *anyone* at Rufftown Street School. It was like inviting them to do the opposite, which Bimbo did. She touched it. She pointed it at her face, pressed the green bulb and a puff of exotic, fragrant perfume wafted out – and paralysed her!

'Crumbs! Wot 'appened?' Doris asked, grabbing the bottle as it fell from Bimbo's stiff little fingers to have a go herself.

One puff later and there were *two* paralysed pupils standing like stone statues beside Edith.

'What *is* this?' she murmured, noticing that the label on the bottle now read '98'. 'What's going on?'

Sweeney suddenly appeared on the platform in front of her. 'Begorrah, tomorrow! But didn't I tell ye to use yer bottle? Now didn't I?'

'So . . . so that's what you meant?' Edith said. '*This* bottle? But why has it changed from "100" to "98"? And how *can* it change?'

'Bejavers, but haven't two o' the squirts been used out o' it?' He grinned, then blew, and popped, another bubble from his bubble-gum. 'Sure now, the bottle contained a hundred little squirts – for the hundred *little squirts* who were annoying ye!' He laughed heartily at his joke.

Edith pointed to the statue-like girls. 'But – are they all right?'

'To be sure. They're only hypnotized. They'll do whatever ye tell 'em!'

'Oh, they will, will they?' Edith turned to them. 'Sit on your chairs, quietly – and behave yourselves.' She turned back to Sweeney. 'I'll fix the others when they return. But, in the meantime, explain yourself. I take it you're the genie of the bottle? Is that it?'

The little green teenybopper leprechaun/genie nodded. 'Sort of.'

'And no one else can see or hear you?' Edith asked. 'Just me?'

'Sure now, only the person with the bottle, Missis.'

'Don't tell me I've got three wishes?' Edith smiled. 'Genies with bottles *always* grant you three wishes! Or is that just in stories?'

'Not wishes – squirts from me bottle,' Sweeney grinned. 'And it depends how many ye need. *You* needed a hundred. So – get squirtin'! Here they come . . .'

The sudden din outside the gymnasium doors signalled the return of the others, so Edith hurried over to meet them. As they entered one by one, she squirted perfume at them, hypnotized them and told them to pick up, and sit quietly on, their chairs. And they obeyed her – like little angels!

'Ninety-nine down and one to go!' she muttered, as Ruffian appeared in the doorway.

'Wot's goin' on in 'ere? Why's everyone quiet? Wot's wrong wiv 'em?'

'I've silenced them,' Edith said. 'And you're next.'

'Wot?' Ruffian gave a burst of laughter. 'No one silences *me*. The teachers can't, they're scared of me. So's the Head. I can do wot I like, see?'

'That's what you think,' said Edith. She pressed the bulb once more, gave Ruffian the last squirt from the bottle and watched the number on the label change from '1' to '0'.

'Hey, you can't do . . .' Ruffian began, but never finished. He stood still, petrified, like his fellow-pupils.

Edith then ordered them all to clear up the gymnasium and put away the equipment they had taken out, then she marched them, in silence, into the playground. There she put them to work clearing up the heaps of litter and rusting bikes, and scrubbing the graffiti and gang slogans off the walls.

'Bejavers and quavers! Ye're doing a grand job, so you are, Missis!'

Edith smiled up at Sweeney, who hovered on his magic carpet above the school gate. 'Tell me, do Irish leprechauns – sorry, genies! – *really* say "begorrah" and "bejavers" and "to be sure" and things like that?'

'We-ell, not really,' he grinned, 'but folks expect ye to talk like that, if ye're Oirish. And I don't like disappointing them!'

Edith suddenly realized she was being stared at. She swung round and saw the puzzled looks on the faces of the Head and Miss Yuill, as they hurried towards her, wondering who on earth she was talking to – on top of the school gate!

Behind them, Edith could see that every window of the school was packed with pupils and teachers, staring out in astonishment at the unlikely – the impossible! – sight of Ruffian and his mates clearing up litter and graffiti.

'But – how did you manage it?' the Head asked. 'We've been trying to get those louts . . . er . . . pupils to clear up their rubbish for ages. You're a genius!'

'It was a gen*ie*, rather than a gen*ius*!' Edith murmured quietly, then added, louder: 'Oh, you just have to use your "bottle", that's all!'

She gathered Ruffian, Doris, Bimbo and their mates together and gave them their final instructions: 'You'll see that the school remains tidy and free of graffiti *and* you'll see that the other pupils keep it that way too. Right?'

'Right, Miss,' they chorused meekly, as the Head shook his head in utter amazement.

'And is it too much to ask you to behave yourselves in future and do as your teachers tell you?'

'No, Miss. Yes, Miss. Whatever you say, Miss!' chanted Ruffian and the rest obediently.

Edith Bolton left the school smiling. She had reformed the wildest school's wildest pupils in a single morning, single-handed – with a little help from her friend Sweeney, of course! And she had also solved the problem of finding an idea for that story her publisher wanted. What else but the story of Sweeney, the Irish genie?

But when she opened her handbag to have another look at the mysterious bottle – it had vanished!

'To be sure, it's someone else's turn for it, now.'

Sweeney suddenly appeared – then disappeared again. 'But – the top o' the morning to ye, Missis!'

So where would the perfume-bottle with the magic properties – and Sweeney – turn up next?

No one knows. But if ever *you* are in need of help, just look out for an old-fashioned green perfume spray-bottle, with a number written on the label. And look out for Sweeney, its teenage Irish genie. He'll be around . . . !

What is hundreds and hundreds of years old, but always nearly new?

The Temple of the Sun Goddess at Ise, in Japan. It is thirteen hundred years old, but every twenty-four years it is taken to pieces and re-built with fresh timber and thatch, exactly the same as it was before. This has been done sixty times so far.

PATRICIA MILES

FOOL'S GOLD

Nicholas Fisk

The Count de Saint-Germain is said to appear every hundred years. He was in Paris in the 1780s, where he told people he had met the Queen of Sheba. In the 1880s the Order of the Golden Dawn claimed him as one of their living members. So perhaps he is due to appear again in the 1980s.

The Ultratech Superbrain Mk III cost £31.50 – all Nat's tenth-birthday money and most of his savings as well. An aunt gave him money to buy an extra memory chip.

Nat followed the blurred instructions, linked his new computer to the TV and switched on. The Ultratech worked. It did sums, told jokes. Later, when Nat's father (who knew about computers) came home, they had the Ultratech doing graphics.

Then tragedy. The Ultratech sizzled – gave off a cloud of smoke – and made a filthy smell. Nat's father said, 'Oh well, the TV's not damaged, that's the main thing.' But Nat was white-faced and miserable.

Next day was Saturday – not a school day. So Nat took his computer back to the shop it came from, Electronix. The shop had a lot going on in the window: disco lights, hi-fi, TVs, everything. The owner, Mr Ronnie, wore a shirt with wide stripes and a brass belt buckle in the form of a smiling face. BE HAPPY!, it said.

Mr Ronnie lived up to this motto when Nat explained about the computer disaster. He jigged about snapping his fingers to the music blaring from two great loudspeakers. 'Yeah,' he said

124

cheerfully. 'Given us a whole lot of trouble, the Ultratech. Load of grief.'

'But it's my birthday present!' Nat said, almost in a howl. He was near to tears.

For a moment, Mr Ronnie stopped jigging and being happy. 'Ah, well, you know how it is,' he said. 'Shortage of staff. Difficulty finding qualified personnel spares-and-service-wise.' He nodded at a felt-penned notice on a door behind the counter. The notice read,

MAINTENANCE & REPAIR DEPT
UCAN RELIONUS!

'We're down to one man,' said Mr Ronnie. 'Waiting list long as your arm. Still, leave it with us –'

At that moment, the telephone rang and Mr Ronnie answered it, forgetting Nat. The caller was someone with a strong sense of grievance. Mr Ronnie began to sweat as loud words poured out at him.

Nat silently and carefully wormed his way past Mr Ronnie. Clutching the Ultratech Superbrain Mk III, he opened the door and entered the Repair Dept.

The place was a mess. Most of the Repair Dept was filled with packing cases, all new; and TV and radio sets, all old. A long, sagging bench under the dirty window was cluttered with meters and tools. Soldering seemed to be the main activity of the place. The bench and wooden floor under it were spattered with silver droplets of solder, as if a metal man had caught a metal cold and couldn't stop sneezing. But the room was empty of men, metal or otherwise.

Then the door opened and a man came in.

The man was slender, handsome, dirty, oddly dressed, bright-eyed and old.

125

He was so old that the hair flowing from his temples looked like the finest threads of white nylon.

Ignoring Nat, this man shuffled rapidly to the bench and lit a cigarette with a soldering iron. 'Oh, filth!' he said. 'Oh, shame! A fool at one end, a fire at the other!' Nat understood that he was talking about his smoking habit. 'Sit down,' the man told Nat. Then he said words in a foreign language. He made Nat nervous.

'Are you foreign, then?' Nat said at last.

'Foreign!' the man said, looking at Nat for the first time. His eyes were like broken jewels, shattered with age. He seemed delighted by Nat's question. 'Foreign! Yes, I am foreign. But only to this century, you understand? Put me in almost any other time, any other circumstance, and I would be at home!'

While Nat was still trying to work out what these words meant, the man blew smoke through his nostrils and said, 'What is your name?'

'Nat.'

'Nat! That is excellent! Brief and to the point! For me, it is more complicated. I will tell you some of my names . . .

'First, I am the Count of Saint-Germain. You like that? No? Then let us try some more names.

'I am also the Margrave of Brandenburg; General Welldone; and Prince Rakoczy. No, let me finish! – I am a Mason of the Fourth Grade; one of the Hidden Masters of Tibet; and have had the honour to be the close, even intimate, friend of the Queen of Sheba. *Voilà!* You may address me as "Count".'

'Actually,' Nat said, 'I came to get this computer mended.'

'I am also known,' said the Count, 'as Froggie, Frenchy and Old Parleyvoo. I do not mind, not at all. You have a saying, I think – "What will it matter in a hundred years' time?"'

'About my computer –'

'"What will it matter in a hundred years' time"!' the Count

said, silencing Nat with a finger like a lizard's claw. 'Oh, I could tell you, my young friend! Oh, my dear young friend, I could answer you!'

Nat said, 'Yes . . . well . . . you're very old, then?'

Once again, he seemed to have said the right thing. The Count excitedly said, 'Guess how old! Come, name me a figure! Sixty, would you say? Seventy, eighty, ninety?'

'Sixty,' said Nat. (He was thinking, 'About ninety.')

'Why not a hundred? Say a hundred! To oblige me, a hundred!'

'A hundred,' Nat said wearily.

'And another hundred! A hundred and a hundred!'

'Look,' Nat said, 'That's why I bought this *computer*. To do sums and things.'

'Sums!' said the Count, almost spitting the word. 'Sums are for silly children! Sums are nothing! The mysteries lie not in sums, but in *numbers*!'

'I want my computer mended,' Nat said.

'Ach! Give it to me, the poor thing . . .'

The Count attacked the computer's casing with screwdrivers, a penknife blade and his own horny, tobacco-stained fingernails. In seconds, he spilled the machine's little glittering guts on the bench.

'The mystic numbers!' cried the Count, his fingers working like lightning on the computer. 'Oh, I could tell you, show you . . . A certain magic square of numbers . . . the pyramid of numbers and the numbers contained in the Pyramids of Egypt . . . the numbers of Good and Evil – there is a number for Evil itself, how well I know that number!'

He probed, jabbed and flicked at the computer as he talked. 'Such rubbish, this machine! No, I do not mean that, it is a nice machine, you are a nice boy . . . There! This chip, always the same chip, there is your trouble. And here is the cure. So . . . I solder him in place . . . Done! *Voilà!* There, happy child, your toy is mended! It will do sums for you once more! But if it could teach you *numbers*, certain *numbers* . . .'

But Nat was looking at the man, not at the machine. 'You're not really two hundred, are you?' he said. 'I mean, that's impossible!'

'No, I am not two hundred,' said the Count, looking straight into Nat's eyes. 'Not two, four, six, eight hundred, either. Older by far! Older by far!'

His eyes seemed to Nat to burn and grow. Nat felt dizzy. 'Do I owe you any money?' he said. He wanted to escape.

'I am paid already.' The Count waved his hand at the dirt and clutter surrounding him.

'Well, would you like some chocolate? I've got this bar . . .' He held out the chocolate.

The Count flinched back. 'I do not eat,' he said.

'But you must. Everyone's got to eat –!'

'I am not everyone. I am the Count of Saint-Germain.'

'But how do you keep alive if you don't eat?'

'My elixir,' the Count replied. 'A liquid. A golden liquid. It is my food, my drink. I discovered it – oh, I cannot remember when, it was in the time of Louis Quinze, Emperor of France. I played with chemistry in those days. It was the fashionable thing, the ladies of the Court loved it. But I played to *win*. The Elixir of Eternity . . .'

'Seriously: how old are you?' Nat said.

The Count tapped out a series of numbers on Nat's computer. They showed on the screen of a TV set.

'That's no answer!' Nat said. 'That's just a string of numbers!'

'Dates,' said the Count. 'Study them. Those dates are like the main courses in the feast of my life. And the feast goes on and on as the centuries roll. Perhaps it goes on for ever.'

'For ever?' Nat said. 'You can't mean that!'

'Perhaps I do not. Let us talk about metals. All metals corrode, rust, decay, die. All but one: gold. I am as gold.'

'Gold!' said Nat. The word itched his mind.

'There were people called alchemists . . .' he said. 'We were told about them at school. They said they could turn base metals into gold.'

'So you know about the alchemists!' said the Count. 'Good boy! Clever boy! Such fools they were, with their signs and symbols and funny hats! Yet not such fools if you pile all their bits of knowledge one on top of the other. Which is what I did.'

'And you made gold?' Nat whispered.

The itch in his mind became burning greed. Gold! – and the pleasures and treasures it could bring! Gold and the Elixir – with its promise of many lifetimes in which to enjoy the power and glory of gold! A proper computer. In a few years, a superbike. A swimming pool in the garden. And then, in the golden future –

'Nonsense!' he told himself. But his mind shimmered with the word *Gold*.

As if reading his mind, the Count said. 'There were golden times for me! Oh, yes! Once, my young friend, I led the conquering army of the Holy Russian Empire! Ah, my horse, my white horse! He slept beside me on a pile of the Empress's furs and woke me in the morning with little kisses! With such a horse, who cares for gold?'

'You wouldn't be working here if you had gold,' Nat said. 'I bet you haven't got any gold, not even a gold ring!'

The Count shrugged, smiled and said 'Pull!'

Hidden in the neck of his shirt was a chain. Nat pulled it. The chain heaped itself in smooth, glistening, heavy loops in the palm of his left hand. Solid gold! Unmistakably gold!

At the end of the chain there hung a flask, a little jade thing encrusted with jewels set in gold. 'You have heard of Cellini?

No? Never mind,' said the Count. 'He lived many hundreds of years ago in the time of the Renaissance. A golden time, a marvellous age. This flask is the work of Cellini's hand – his own hand. I saw him apply these enamels. In the days of the Renaissance . . .'

'But you could make gold!' Nat whispered. 'Actually make gold! You could, couldn't you?'

Again the Count shrugged. 'But Cellini,' he said, 'could make *this*.'

Mister Ronnie staggered in carrying a huge, ugly TV set. 'Rush job!' he shouted. 'Belongs to a friend of the wife's! Top priority! Get cracking!' He hurried out.

The Count lifted an eyebrow at Nat and said, 'Ah, well. To serious matters. A friend of the wife's!' He reached for a screwdriver.

Nat said, 'No, please! Listen to me! About making gold – tell me! You don't need gold any more, you're old –'

The Count began laughing, like a big bird crowing. 'It is merely a sum,' he said. 'A sum – a formula – a recipe – an equation. You are a good boy, a clever boy, you do not need sums. There is more in you than that.' Already his incredibly fast, incredibly clever fingers had stripped off the back of the TV and applied clips from a meter to parts of its insides.

'*Please!*' said Nat. 'The formula or whatever it is! Tell me!'

The Count lit a cigarette – his laughter made him sputter smoke; took Nat's computer; and tapped its little keys.

'There, silly boy,' he said, quite kindly and softly. 'Now you must go. I have serious work to do. The friend of the wife's TV!'

'Have you done it, then?' Nat said. 'Given me the formula?'

'Of course.'

'Just that short number you tapped out? That's really it? To make gold?'

'Of course. Run along and make your gold.'

Nat ran. Left alone, the Count of Saint-Germain crouched over the TV set, smiling and nodding in a cloud of cigarette smoke as he solved the simple mystery of repairing it.

Nat ran home and almost flung himself and his computer at the TV set.

'Hey, none of that!' his mother said. 'You're off to Billy's for the weekend, remember? And you're late. Eat your lunch in the car. Come on, now! I'll pick you up about nine, Sunday night.'

Nat had quite forgotten. He felt sick.

When at last he got home, the computer was waiting for him. He linked it to the TV, fed in the program and watched the screen come alive.

An equation appeared. It made no sense. There were ordinary numbers, but also little pictures and symbols.

The computer seemed to understand. Soon the equation was blanked out and replaced with another, longer one made of ordinary numbers.

'Good!' Nat muttered. 'More!'

The computer produced a third equation: then a fourth and fifth –

And then, at dazzling speed, another and another and another until the screen exploded with rushing images –

And all at once, the screen was gold, pure gold –

Then the Ultratech sizzled – gave off a cloud of smoke – and made a filthy smell.

The TV screen turned its usual luminous grey.

For the first time in his life, Nat played truant. On Monday he went to Electronix instead of school. He got there as

131

Mr Ronnie finished sticking a notice to the shop door: EXPERIENCED REPAIRMAN WANTED URGENTLY.

'So he's gone?' Nat said. Somehow, he knew the Count would not be there.

'Yeah, gone. Left a note: "I am returning to the Renaissance." Stupid old –'

Nat silently held out his computer. Mr Ronnie said, 'You think *you've* got troubles! All right, then . . . Hand it over. Can't promise anything. Where's the Renaissance, then? South of France? Sounds Frenchy.'

Mr Ronnie inspected his notice. Nat prepared to leave. Mr Ronnie said, 'Here, hang on. Keep this, it'll only get lost.' He threw the computer's extra memory to Nat.

The little plastic thing felt strangely heavy in Nat's hand. Impossibly heavy.

Nat's father pulled the memory to pieces; and took the insides to Mason's the Jewellers.

Mason's whistled, scratched their heads and handed over enough money to buy Nat a microcomputer with 32K of random access and full-colour graphic facilities.

For the memory turned out to be pure gold.

THE VISIT

Joan G. Robinson

'I'll wait for you here,' said Auntie Pat, whose real name was Miss Corby.

'You don't have to specially,' said Rosa gruffly. She hoped her voice sounded convincing.

They were in a teashop, quite a long way from home. They had come on a bus and a train. Rosa had been looking forward to this visit for weeks, months, years, it seemed. She had jolly well worked for it too, she thought, looking sideways under her lashes at Auntie Pat carefully not looking at her. She had started by asking for it, then pleading, then nagging. But Auntie Pat – who had been her foster-mother for years and years – had fobbed her off with some excuse every time. Rosa had played her up no end then, she remembered. Sometimes she had *hated* her.

But at last Rosa had got her way. The visit had been arranged, and now it was happening! They were almost there. No wonder she felt a bit scary. It wasn't every day you went to meet your own mother for the first time.

She pushed back her chair and stood up. Staring at the chocolate éclairs in the window, which she had refused, she said, 'Do the others know?' Miss Corby shook her head.

'Only Mrs Taylor. She had to know, being on duty. The children probably think you've gone to the dentist.'

Rosa made a face, nearly smiled, then turned sharply to the door and went out. Auntie Pat was taking it well, she thought, considering she had lost the battle. But it wouldn't do to let her know. She might want to come all the way then. 'I'll go alone,'

Rosa had said all along. 'I don't want *you* there, listening to everything.'

She walked along the two short roads to her mother's house, remembering some of the things Auntie Pat had said to put her off. *You know, Rosa, just because somebody was your mother doesn't make them automatically wonderful. It isn't a magic.* Well, of course it wasn't. She knew that. But her own mum might still be a sight more wonderful than Auntie Pat would ever be. Younger probably, with a smooth kind face and soft wavy hair – not frizzy horsehair anyway – and nice understanding brown eyes. *And she could be a very ordinary person, you know, Rosa –* with a certain emphasis on the 'very'. Well, of course. Rosa was old enough now to know her mum wasn't likely to be a film star or a princess, or even a telly announcer as she had once believed. But at least she wouldn't be an ordinary boring foster-mother with a crowd of snotty-nosed kids trailing after her.

The house was a small square bungalow, very neat and empty-looking. Rosa walked up the path and rang the bell before she could lose her nerve. Then she stood waiting. She had no idea what to expect. It couldn't be a case of a hug, surely? Not yet. But to shake hands wouldn't seem quite right. Perhaps a kiss then? As it happened it was none of these. The door was opened suddenly by a tall, bony woman with shiny red cheeks and straight hair scraped tightly back into a knot at the back of her head. She was wearing a clean cotton apron. The folds where it had been ironed still showed.

'Yes?' she said, and glared down at Rosa.

'Are you – are you Mrs Dunn?' Rosa asked, pretty sure she was not.

'You *could* call me that,' said the woman cautiously. 'What d'you want?'

'I'm Rosa – your daughter.' It sounded silly now.

'Oh.' The woman stared at her in silence for a long moment.

Then she said in a slightly more amiable tone, 'You'd better come in then.'

Rosa followed her into a small bleak-looking room, only sparsely furnished but spotlessly clean. There was hideously patterned lino on the floor, and one very small woollen rug, barely the size of a doormat. They sat on hard chairs, facing each other and trying to smile. Rosa's face felt like cardboard.

'They told me you might come,' said her mother. 'But I didn't think you would. Not really –' She fell silent and began picking at her apron. Rosa was dismayed. She almost looks frightened of me, she thought.

'Aren't you pleased?' she asked, and heard her voice rise to a squeak on the last word. She coughed to cover it.

Mrs Dunn shifted uneasily on her chair. 'Well – yes, of course,' she said doubtfully, 'but there's more to it than that.' She gave a quick glance round. 'I mean I ain't got the room here, have I? That's what I told Miss Whatsername.'

Rosa stiffened. Blimey, she was thinking, you don't kill yourself trying to look pleased to see me, do you! You *bloody* well don't! There was no question of crying now. Mrs Dunn must have sensed her anger. She leaned forward on her chair.

'Look after you all right, do they?' Rosa nodded, too full to speak. 'That's all right then. More'n I'd ever 'ave been able to do.'

'Why wouldn't you?' Rosa demanded.

Mrs Dunn gave a short sharp laugh. 'Kids ain't *my* line!' – She seemed surprised at the question – 'Never were. Anyway I'd 'ave lost my job if I'd took you along – anyway it'd 'ave been difficult all ways round –' Her voice trailed away. Rosa waited. A sudden look of suspicion crept into Mrs Dunn's eyes. 'They put you up to coming, did they? What would they want from *me* after all these years, eh? Tell me that.'

Rosa shook her head fiercely. 'No. No. Nobody told me. I

135

came because I wanted to see you, that's all.' She took a sudden risk and added, 'Didn't you ever want to see me?'

Mrs Dunn considered. 'Can't honestly say I did. When you was born of course, I did then. You was a nice little baby. But it wasn't no use after, when I knew you'd be going. Best gone and forgotten then, I said. And that's what I still say.' Then, seeing the expression on Rosa's face, she added, 'But don't get me wrong. I don't bear you no hard feelings. You couldn't help coming when you did.'

Rosa's eyes grew wider in astonishment. 'When do you mean? Now? Or when I was born?'

'A bit o' both, I should think,' said Mrs Dunn. 'Anyway I learned the rules then and I've gone by 'em ever since. Keep your trap shut, keep your nose clean, and mind your own business. That's about it.'

There seemed nothing more to say after that. Rosa wondered whether she ought to get up and go. Was that what her mother wanted? But she felt stuck to the chair. She forced herself to forget all the things she had dreamed might happen on this day, and thought only of this minute. Was she going to be offered a cup of tea? She hoped not. Mrs Dunn seemed stuck to her chair too. Why didn't she ask Rosa things, what it was like where she lived, had she any friends? Either there was everything to talk about, or nothing. Nothing, it seemed.

She got up, mumbling that someone was waiting for her, and she mustn't stay. Her mother looked up sharply.

'Waiting for you?'

'Yes, Miss Corby. We call her Auntie Pat.'

Mrs Dunn nodded with a knowing look. 'That'll be her what come here. The way she was ferreting around asking questions I thought maybe she was thinking of placing you here.'

Rosa, appalled at the idea, assured her she was not.

'That's all right then.' Mrs Dunn seemed relieved. 'I must say you've been luckier than what I was. A nice home, she

136

said, and only ten of you. More like a family, she said. She seemed a nice lady. There was more'n a hundred where I was.'

'Were you a *homes* girl?' asked Rosa, surprised.

'Course I was, but not much *home* about it. A blooming great orphanage it was, no foster-ma's or "aunties" for us.'

'But more than a *hundred*?' said Rosa, unbelieving. 'All with no families of their own?'

'Well, o' course,' said Mrs Dunn. She pointed a finger at her. 'Don't you go thinking you're special just because you ain't got no family. There's hundreds and hundreds what ain't. More, I shouldn't wonder. Stands to reason when you think of it, what with all the traffic, and wars on the telly and things.'

Ten minutes later, pausing to get her breath in a doorway, Rosa could see Auntie Pat in the teashop over the road. She was bending forward, peering into the teapot, which surely must be empty by now! How dear and ordinary she looked. Rosa felt a catch in her throat. And to think she had imagined she might be jealous of Rosa's beautiful and wonderful mother!

'Oh, cripes!' she muttered, and dashed across the road.

'*Careful!*' said a man on a bike.

'Sorry,' said Rosa, and ran on. Auntie Pat saw her coming. Her eyes lit up. 'All right?' they seemed to say.

Rosa nodded, smiled, and put out a hand. 'I'll tell you on the bus.' She glanced at the éclairs. 'Can I have one now?'

THE OLD HUNDREDTH

Leon Garfield

Every good story begins with a journey . . . even if it's only to a churchyard, as the soldier said when the general choked on a fishbone.

'If you want to look round,' offered the girl who was standing on the corner, 'I'll be 'appy to show you.'

She pointed down an opening between a public house and a

20 trees

138

furniture factory, that gaped like a beggar's pocket. I shuddered and shook my head.

'Come on,' she urged, smoothing her flowery cotton dress and sniffing as if she had an ancient cold she was fond of. 'We're a settlement. Religious. Come 'ere more'n two 'undred years ago. We're educational. Schools come. Teachers and all. Honest.'

I saw that the pocket had a hole in it, and I caught a glimpse of a tree and some brick cottages, dozing in the evening sun.

'It won't cost you nothin',' promised the girl. 'And I'd be much obliged.'

She was about fourteen, with sturdy legs, straw-coloured hair, and a face as pale as bread. I didn't much like the look of

+100 years

her. But then I don't much like any young people. They're a
bad lot. They're always wanting something; usually money.
You can see it in their greedy eyes. Hers were as wide open as
starlings' beaks; and just as sharp.

'Come on, mister,' she pleaded. 'You won't 'ave to pay
nothin'. Cross me 'eart and 'ope to fry!'

It was very awkward. People were passing and I didn't want
them to think me mean.

'All right,' I said; and she fairly skipped with delight.
'Whatever it is that you want,' I thought, as I walked with her
towards the hole in the pocket, 'you're not going to get it,
young lady!'

She smelled strongly of old-fashioned carbolic soap. I had to

+220 volts

admit that she was unnaturally clean for her age. Even her fingernails, I noticed, were as white as paper.

'We started off,' she informed me, as we passed between a pair of gate-posts from which the gates had long since fallen away, ''undreds an' 'undreds of years ago, somewhere just off Czechoslovakia. We was gettin' burnt,' she explained, as if there'd been an accident in the kitchen, 'by the Pope; so we 'ad to flee. Then we wandered about a bit, preachin' an' suchlike, till we come over 'ere an' settled.'

She waved her arm about her to show me. I looked, and saw that we had stepped inside a peaceful little world of discreet trees that spoke in whispers, a quiet square, and two or three short streets that were all quilted with cobbles, so that one

+1,000 cc

seemed to be walking over a sea of stony bubbles. She showed me the terraced cottages, the school, the doctor's house, the watchman's house, and the church whose deeply worn steps spoke of an ever-loyal congregation.

'We done it all ourselves,' she said. 'We even made the bricks.'

They looked it. They were all shapes and sizes and speckled with black, like children's rock-cakes. You never saw such home-made-looking bricks.

'We got everythin' 'ere,' she said proudly. 'No need to go outside at all. We even got our own buryin' ground. Come an' 'ave a look.'

+30,000 *therms*

Her voice trembled a little, and her greedy eyes almost yawned at me. 'Whatever it is you're after,' I thought again, 'you're not going to get it from me, young lady!'

She took me to the churchyard and waited, with all the importance of a real lady, for me to open the gate. Then she skipped inside and I followed.

It was a strange churchyard. It was really an orchard that had been planted with apple trees, pear trees . . . and people. There was a sundial in the middle, but as the branches overhead were as muddled as string, no sunshine got through, so time stood still.

The gravestones themselves were as strange as the church-

+1,000,000 people

yard. They were no more than oblong tablets, about the size of wedding albums, laid out neatly on either side of a path, as if ready for an enormous game of dominoes.

'Ladies on one side an' gents on the other,' said the girl cheerfully. 'But we're all sisters an' brothers under the sod.' Then she frowned as one stone, that was a good two inches bigger than its neighbours, caught her eye. 'But there's always some,' she muttered darkly, 'as will always push themselves forward, no matter where.'

I didn't like the way she spoke. I thought it was very disrespectful. But as it wasn't my place to tell her, I ignored her remark and said that it seemed unkind for wives and husbands to be separated for ever, even if only by a path.

+760.98 mph

'Oh, no,' she protested. 'They say that, after dark, we all comes out an' strolls about a bit.'

'Even when it's raining?'

'Better'n ever. They say that, when it's wet, we comes over all shiny.'

She stared at me unblinkingly, as if challenging me to say that she'd made it up. She was, I thought, a very impudent girl; and I liked her even less. She shrugged her shoulders, and then, as if I wasn't there, she began hopping from gravestone to gravestone, as high, sudden and flowery as a bridesmaid frog.

'Tread on a nick, An' you'll marry a brick,' she chanted, as she played her grim game of hopscotch: 'An' a beetle will come to your weddin'!'

+130 decibels

She halted, balancing on one leg.

'Come an' 'ave a look!' she called.

I picked my way respectfully among the graves and joined her. The stone she was standing on was engraved, 'Number One. Hannah Schwarz. 1790. M.S.'

'She was the first of us to fall asleep,' said the girl, 'so she's Number One.'

'What's M.S.?'

'Married Sister, of course! Number Two's over the other side. Joseph Schwarz, M.B. That's for Married Brother. 'E went in the same year.'

She laughed and hopped off Hannah Schwarz on to Number Three, a Single Sister; and then, with a tremendous jump that

+100,000 sq. feet of office space

frightened the butterflies into flying scraps of paper, she landed on Number Six . . .

'We goes all the way down to eight 'undred an' seventy-five!' she boasted, as she hopped gaily, first on one foot, then on the other, from sleeping Sister to sleeping Sister; while on the other side the Brothers slumbered undisturbed.

'Tread on a nick,
An' you'll marry a brick,
An' a beetle will come to your weddin'!'
Suddenly she halted, still as a bird.

''Ere's a good 'un!' she said. 'Come an' 'ave a look.'

She was perched on Number Ninety-nine. Rebecca Forlorn. 1892. G.G.

+10,000 megatons

'What's G.G.?'

'Great Girl, of course! We're all Great Girls till we're fifteen. Then we get to be Sisters.'

'Well, you're certainly a Great Girl,' I thought. 'A great greedy lump of a girl with no more respect for the dead than for the living!'

Her eyes were enormous with wanting. I glanced down at the stone next to her. It was Number One Hundred and Three. As I have a tidy mind, I walked over to the other side, to find Number One Hundred. There wasn't one. There was a space next to Number Ninety-eight, then there was Number One Hundred and One.

'Where is Number One Hundred?' I asked.

=125,975,040 *acres of room for improvement*

She shrugged her shoulders, and scraped her toe on Number Ninety-nine.

'There was a lot of us what went in 1892,' she said, taking no notice of my question. 'It was on account of the cholera. It was brung in from the butcher's shop down the road. In next to no time, we was dropping down fast as leaves. One moment we was bright as ninepence, and the next, we was dead as a penny.'

'Including Number One Hundred?'

'We used to light a candle in the winder,' she went on, treating my question as if, like the mysterious One Hundred, it didn't exist, 'so's the watchman could see we was sick. Then 'e'd go for the doctor, 'oo'd come an' poke 'is nose round the door, take a good look an' a good sniff, an' say, "God rest 'er soul! Best bury 'er quick an' scrub out the 'ouse with carbolic!"'

'But why isn't there a Number One Hundred?' I repeated, beginning to grow angry at the way I was being ignored.

'Sometimes, though,' said the girl, as if I hadn't spoken, 'they was a bit too quick off the mark. With the buryin', I mean. There we'd be, prayers said, the 'ole dug, and us wakin' up in the coffin, bright as ninepence! You 'ad to laugh!'

'Did you!' I thought. 'Well, it's not my idea of a joke!' She began to fidget. She shivered. She looked quickly about her, as if she'd heard someone coming to fetch her.

'Come on!' she said suddenly. 'It's time to go!'

'Why?'

'It's gettin' dark.'

It was indeed. Night had crept into the churchyard and was making shadowy giants of the trees. The sundial was crouching like a mourner, and the air was heavy with the threat of rain.

'Ninety-nine, 'op!' she cried, skipping off Rebecca Forlorn. 'You Great Girl, you!'

She ran out of the churchyard so quickly that I suspected she was frightened of being caught and punished. I followed, remembering to shut the gate. I didn't expect to see her again, as I thought that she'd gone home. But there she was, standing in the deeply shadowed square, watching for me with eyes that seemed to have swallowed up her face.

'Look!' she whispered eagerly. 'Just look at that!'

She pointed; and it seemed that even as I looked, a window in a cottage winked into a tottering yellow life.

'It's a candle!' she said; and her voice was shrill with excitement. ''E must be ill!'

I said we'd better go at once and get some help.

'It's only old Isaac Candy!' she chuckled. 'Come on! Let's go and 'ave a look!'

Poor Isaac Candy! I thought; to have your beacon of distress seen by such heartless eyes! She skipped across the square towards the lighted window as if she was gathering nuts in May, instead of going to sickness in September. She reached the window and pressed her face against the glass as eagerly and greedily as if she was looking into a sweetshop.

'There 'e is!' she whispered, as I came up beside her. 'Sittin' in 'is old chair calm as Christmas!'

I looked into the little parlour. It was so small that, had the window been open, I could have reached inside and touched the ornaments on the mantelpiece, and even the pictures on the wall. There was an armchair drawn up before the fireplace; and in it was an old, old man. He was so withered and wrinkled and crumpled and creased that, as he sat in his chair, he looked like a dried-up kernel in a shabby old shell. His eyes were shut, his mouth was open, and his arms hung down by his sides. He was as still as a photograph. He was dead.

''E's gone all right,' said the girl, nodding. 'An' about time too.'

I stared at her in amazement. I could not believe that even a fourteen-year-old could be so unfeeling! She looked back at me, suddenly anxious.

'After all,' she said, by way of excusing herself, ''e were aged a 'undred and seven. It were time enough for 'im to go.'

'We'd better call the neighbours,' I said, 'and fetch a doctor.'

'What for?' she asked. ''E'll keep till mornin'. Come on! Let's 'ave a look inside!'

Before I could stop her, she'd opened the door and slipped inside the old man's cottage! If there'd been a policeman near, I'd have called him; but there was no one. I was about to go and knock up the neighbours, when the girl called to me.

'Please don't go away, mister! Please come inside and 'elp me. I'd be much obliged.'

Her voice sounded frightened, and even desperate; and I remembered that she was, after all, little more than a child. I went into the cottage. It stank of old food, old tobacco, old clothes and old age. The girl was halfway up the narrow stairs.

'It's up 'ere. That's where 'e keeps it. It's under 'is bed.'

She vanished and I followed her. I feared that the old man had kept his money, or some silver, under his bed, and that she was planning to steal it.

She'd gone into his bedroom, which was even smaller than his parlour, and was on her hands and knees beside the bed.

'It's there all right!' she cried excitedly. 'It's in 'is box! Give us a 'and, mister, I can't manage it meself!' Then she looked up at me. 'Please!' she said. 'I'd be much obliged!'

I bent down, and pulled out a heavy wooden box that was tied up with cord.

'Open it!' she begged, shaking all over with excitement. 'Open it up, mister, an' let's 'ave a look inside!'

I untied the cord and lifted up the lid. The box was stuffed with old newspapers, and an ancient musty smell. I took out

151

the newspapers until at last I'd uncovered what the box contained.

'There!' sighed the girl, enormously relieved. 'I knew 'e'd still got it!'

The old man's treasure, that he'd kept so jealously hidden from all but the eyes of his Great Girl, was an oblong tablet of stone, about the size of a wedding album. On it was engraved, as freshly as the day it had been done, 'Number One Hundred. Isaac Candy. 1892. G.B.'

'There's your Number One 'Undred, mister,' whispered the girl. 'An' there's me Great Boy! You see, 'e got the cholera an' they thought 'e was gone. They'd dug 'is 'ole an' carved 'is stone. Then 'e come back to life again, bright as ninepence. You really 'ad to laugh!'

She laughed, but I, being both older and younger, felt tears in my eyes. She stood up and moved towards the door.

'I'd be much obliged, mister, if you'd carry 'is stone an' put it where it properly belongs. As you must know, I can't manage it meself.'

I lifted up the stone and carried it down the stairs.

'Much obliged, much obliged!' she called, as she flickered across the square. 'It 'ad to be the old 'un, didn't it! After all, 'oo ever 'eard of a Great Boy, aged a 'undred an' seven!'

I went back to the churchyard and laid the stone in its place, among the Brothers. I couldn't see the girl any more, but I knew that she was in the churchyard.

''E took 'is time,' I heard her say. 'But better late than never!'

It had begun to rain. It was a fine rain that muttered and pattered on the leaves. I could hear a sound of laughter, and then a high, sweet chanting:

'Tread on a nick,

An' I'll marry a brick,

An' a beetle will come to our weddin'! Oh you Great Boy, you! Fancy keepin' me waitin' all this time!'

'Well, young lady,' I murmured, 'you got what you wanted after all!' I'd been right all the time. The young always want something; only it's not money, it's love.

As I left the churchyard, I thought I saw people shining.

100 PLUS

Gyles Brandreth

100 is a number and a very good number too. Ten 100s make 1,000 and that's another good number. Take 100 and multiply it by 1,000 and you get 100,000 – a really wonderful number, that. Now add just one and you've got 100,001, the most remarkable number of all.

100,001 is capable of fantastic feats. Multiply it by any five-digit number you like and you will get a ten-digit answer made up of the five digits repeated twice. It sounds unlikely but it's true. Watch:

$$100001 \times 12345 = 1234512345$$
$$100001 \times 54321 = 5432154321$$
$$100001 \times 67890 = 6789067890$$
$$100001 \times 98765 = 9876598765$$
$$100001 \times 13579 = 1357913579$$
$$100001 \times 24680 = 2468024680$$
$$100001 \times 99999 = 9999999999$$
$$100001 \times 69696 = 6969669696$$
$$100001 \times 10001 = 1000110001$$

AN OBVIOUS GLIDOGRAM

Ronald Ridout

1 C				
2	R			
3		K		
4			T	
5				E
6			O	
7		I		
8	R			
9 S				

1. There are 100 of them in a dollar

2. A mistake

3. With no clothes on

4. You bite with them

5. To undo string, for example

6. A machine that does human work

7. A very foolish person

8. To rub out

9. Rapid; also a bird

_____ last a hundred years.

A PROVERBIAL GLIDOGRAM

Ronald Ridout

There are hundreds of proverbs: do you know these?

1	E			
2		D		
3			E	
4				E
5					D
6			M	
7			R	
8		N		
9	E			

1. Walls have —

2. — ale is the best brew.

3. Half a loaf is better than no —

4. Sticks and stones may break my —, but words will never hurt me.

5. The pen is mightier than the —

6. Man is his own worst —

7. — of a feather flock together.

8. Better a fool than a —

9. Don't put all your — into one basket.

_____ man will clutch at a straw.

Solutions on page 167

THE PLAGUE OF PEACOCKS

Diana Wynne Jones

From the moment the Platts came to Chipping Hanbury everyone knew they were Caring People. They bought the old cottage up Weavers Close beside the field where the children went to play football and cycle. Mr Platt took the cottage apart all by himself and built it up again and painted it white. Mrs Platt took the garden apart and painted everything there white too.

When they had done that, they began caring for Chipping Hanbury.

Mr Platt brought out a news-sheet which he called *Hanbury Village News* and put a copy through everyone's door. The copies were addressed to everyone by their first names in the most friendly way: the Willises' was to Glenda and Jack, the Moores' to Lily and Tony, the Dougals' to Marcia and Ken, and so on. Everyone wondered how Mr Platt knew, and whether he was right to call Hanbury a village when it was really just a place on the edge of London. The news-sheet was full of kind advice about how Hanbury needed more street lights and a bus shelter and tidier front gardens. Weavers Pond was full of rubbish too, Mr Platt said reproachfully, and the football field ought to be a proper Sports Centre. People like Glenda and Jack, who had private incomes, ought really to see about cleaning the place up.

'Why does he think we have private incomes?' said Mrs Willis. 'Because the children have ponies?' Mrs Willis did typing for people in order to pay for the ponies and she was rather hurt.

Meanwhile, Mrs Platt was caring for animals. The first to go

156

was the Dougals' cat, Sooty. Then the Deans' dog, Lambert. Then Holly Smith's angora rabbit. Mrs Platt called on the Dougals, the Deans and the Smiths and explained at length that she had found the animal wandering about, and it might have gone in the road, and there was such a lot of traffic these days, and one should keep pets tied up. Mrs Platt was thin, with intense grey eyes, and she bent forward nervously when she talked, and twisted her hands together. People found it hard to interrupt her when she was so worried. But after an hour or so, the Dougals and the Deans and the Smiths plucked up courage to ask what had happened to their animals. Mrs Platt explained that she had put them in the car and Mr Platt had driven them to a vet he knew to have them put down.

Mr Platt's next news-sheet had a sorrowful page on how badly people looked after their animals. The other pages were about the new greenhouses Mr Platt was building behind the cottage. Mr Platt was a thick, energetic man with a beard and juicy red lips, and he had a passion for building greenhouses. When he was not doing that, he was either standing with his head back and his chest out admiring the latest greenhouse, or he was walking round Hanbury looking for news to put in his news-sheet. He was walking in Hart Lane when Sarah Willis got run away with by her pony.

What made Chunter bolt was a mystery. Sarah always said he had seen Mr Platt and was afraid of being taken to the vet too. Anyway, there was Chunter hammering along the road, striking frantic sparks from it with his hooves, with Sarah clinging on for dear life, when Mr Platt came jumping out of the hedge and swung on Chunter's bridle.

'Thanks,' said Sarah, when Chunter had stopped.

'You should never, never let a pony gallop on a tarmac road,' said Mr Platt. 'I don't think anyone has explained to you: it ruins their feet and jars their legs.'

'But I didn't –!' said Sarah. That was all she managed to say, because Mr Platt proved to be just as good a talker as his wife, and he walked back to the house with her, holding Chunter's bridle and explaining gently how you should treat a pony. 'I think I must come inside and explain to Glenda that you shouldn't ride out without proper supervision,' he said when they got there. And he did. When he had done that, he went out to look at the barn where the ponies lived and came back to tell Mrs Willis that it was not suitable for ponies.

Mrs Willis was typing somebody's book about the history of Poland, full of names like Mrzchtochky, and she left out several Z's. 'I shall go mad,' she said.

'Don't worry,' said Sarah. 'There's always Daniel Emanuel.'

No one had yet told the Platts about Daniel Emanuel. This was odd, because Daniel Emanuel was well known to be interested in animals too. Only the week before, he had fallen out of the oak-tree in the football field trying to catch a squirrel. Last year he had cut himself on rusty iron wading into Weavers Pond after a duck and nearly died of tetanus, because he had heard you could eat ducks.

Mrs Platt met Daniel Emanuel first, while she was coming home after caring for the Moores' budgie. She had found it on her window-sill. By this time, she had noticed that people did not quite like it when she took their pets to the vet. So she took the budgie home. 'Look, Lily,' she explained, 'I've cut his wings for you, ever so neatly, so that he won't be able to fly away again.'

'How kind!' Mrs Moore said bitterly, thinking she would not have to keep the cat in the yard in case Mrs Platt cared for the cat too. 'You'll have to keep the budgie in your bedroom,' she said to her son Terry. 'I hope Daniel Emanuel does something to the Platts soon!'

Mrs Platt had got halfway home, to the bottom of the main road, when she saw, to her horror, a four-year-old boy walk out into the traffic. A bus bucked to a stop almost on top of him. Two cars missed him by two separate miracles. Mrs Platt rushed into the road and seized the child's arm. 'Who are you, little man? Does your mummy know you're out?'

He looked up at her. 'I'm Daniel Emanuel of course,' he said. He had curly hair and long eyelashes and a band of freckles across his nose.

'Where do you live?' said Mrs Platt.

Daniel Emanuel did not seem to be sure. He let Mrs Platt lead him round Chipping Hanbury. She seemed to want to, and he felt like a walk anyway. After an hour or so though, she began to bother him. She kept asking things and calling him 'little man'. The only little men Daniel Emanuel had ever heard of were the dwarves in Snow White, and he began to be afraid he would not grow any more. He took Mrs Platt home so that he could ask Linda.

Mrs Platt looked at the O'Flahertys' tall ramshackle house with pieces of car lying about the front garden under the washing line. Children were running and screaming, and Mrs O'Flaherty was anxiously looking over the front gate. 'This is a Problem Family,' Mrs Platt said to herself, 'and I must care for them.'

'Daniel Emanuel!' everyone in the garden screamed.

'He was walking in the traffic,' Mrs Platt explained. She had meant to have a long talk with Mrs O'Flaherty about her problems, but Mrs O'Flaherty was so glad to see Daniel Emanuel safe that she took him straight indoors. 'No manners either,' Mrs Platt said sorrowfully.

Indoors, Mrs O'Flaherty said, 'You naughty boy!' and raised her fist. Daniel Emanuel's face screwed up miserably. 'Oh, I can't hit him!' said Mrs O'Flaherty and she took her fist down. Daniel Emanuel unscrewed his face and beamed. 'Linda,' said Mrs O'Flaherty, 'why did you let him go in the road?'

Linda was five, and the only one who knew how to manage Daniel Emanuel. She shrugged. There were times when even she could not stop Daniel Emanuel. 'He can think,' she explained, 'and the cars just stop.'

'He may think they will, but they don't,' said Mrs O'Flaherty and hurried away to get lunch. A mother who has seven children and a husband who spends his spare time stock-car racing has not quite time to understand everything.

'Am I a little man?' Daniel Emanuel asked Linda anxiously.

Linda knew what he meant. 'Not you!' she said. 'You'll grow bigger than Dad.'

Daniel Emanuel was much relieved. He was not sure he liked Mrs Platt. She said things that were not true.

Mr Platt's next news-sheet had a lot in it about Problem Families.

'Oh good,' said Mrs Willis to Sarah and James. 'They've met Daniel Emanuel.'

Next time Daniel Emanuel gave Linda the slip he went to look at the Platts' cottage. He thought it was lovely. The stones round the flowers were painted white. There was a white wheelbarrow on the front lawn with flowers planted in it, which bothered Daniel Emanuel. Flowers grew in the ground. Daniel Emanuel took the flowers out carefully and tipped the earth on the grass. He found Mr Platt's golf clubs in the porch and dug a hole for the flowers with them in front of the porch. He put the flowers in the hole and carefully opened the tap in the rainwater butt to give the flowers a drink. Then he found a pot of white paint in the porch and thought he ought to give the hole a white rim like the other flowerbeds. When Mr Platt came round the house from building his fourth greenhouse, he found Daniel Emanuel squatting in a river using a bent golf club as a paintbrush.

Mr Platt took Daniel Emanuel in a stern, kind hand and led him home, talking gently to him about how wicked he was. Daniel Emanuel seemed a little vague about what wicked meant. Mr Platt explained by telling him stories, and one of the stories was Daniel in the Lions' Den.

'Oh Daniel Emanuel!' said Mrs O'Flaherty when she opened the door. Daniel Emanuel was earth-coloured with streaks of white. Mr Platt was shocked to see Mrs O'Flaherty had been reading a book while she cooked lunch. She had two favourite books which she read turn and turn about to keep her sane: this one was *The Mill on the Floss*, the other was *The Count of Monte Cristo*. She knew both so well that she could do most things while she was reading.

Mr Platt explained what Daniel Emanuel had done and gave Mrs O'Flaherty long and patient advice on how to bring up children, until Mrs O'Flaherty smelt the potatoes burning and snatched Daniel Emanuel up and ran. 'What a feckless woman,' Mr Platt said sadly.

Mrs O'Flaherty was so annoyed about the potatoes that Daniel Emanuel barely got scolded. 'Where's any lions?' he asked Linda as soon as he was free.

'Aren't any,' said Linda. 'Only in cages in the Zoo.'

The next day, Daniel Emanuel set out to find himself a cage of lions.

There are no lions in Chipping Hanbury. The only large beasts are Sarah Willis's Chunter and James Willis's Ben. Daniel Emanuel was seen by James standing in the doorway of the ponies' barn. 'Is this a den?' Daniel Emanuel asked.

'No,' said James. 'It's a stall.'

Daniel Emanuel nodded and went away. He was next heard of eight miles away in Abbots Hanbury. How he got there Daniel Emanuel never said, but there he was. He was in a pen in the cattle market with a hundred pigs, angrily shouting, 'Bite me!' His father was home when the police telephoned. He drove his newest car to Abbots Hanbury and fetched Daniel Emanuel away. Since Mr O'Flaherty was the only person in the world that Daniel Emanuel was afraid of, Daniel Emanuel arrived home very sore and sullen. 'I don't like Platts,' he told Linda.

Both the Platts were very concerned about Daniel Emanuel. Mr Platt went to see Mr O'Flaherty to tell him Daniel Emanuel needed special care, and the Dougals saw him leave again rather quickly. Mrs Platt went to speak to Mrs Willis. 'Glenda,' she said, 'I think we two should get together and care for our Problem Family. The O'Flahertys, you know.'

This time, Mrs Willis was typing someone's experimental novel. It went down the page in two columns which said the same thing, but not quite, and it had to catch the five o'clock post. 'I don't think they're a problem,' she said. 'Ask James and Sarah. Their main friends are Patrick and Thelma O'Flaherty. Do let me catch the post.' But Mrs Platt stayed persuading Mrs Willis till four o'clock. At four-thirty Mr Platt arrived with some brochures, saying that he and Mrs Platt thought Mrs Willis ought to be using a word processor. When Sarah and James and Mr Willis came home just after five, Mr Platt was still there and Mrs Willis was in tears.

'Do something!' said Mr Willis.

James and Sarah saddled the ponies and went drumming away down the bridle-path to the football field where Thelma and Patrick were riding their bicycles. 'What is it?' said Patrick, propping himself on the hedge.

'Make Daniel Emanuel do something to the Platts,' said Sarah.

'You can borrow the ponies and we'll go on a bike-and-pony trek if you do,' said James.

Thelma and Patrick looked wistfully at one another. It was an offer they couldn't refuse. It cost Patrick a lot to say, 'We can't make him do anything.' And it cost Thelma just as much to add, 'Linda's his manager.'

'Ask her, and we'll do the trek anyway,' said Sarah.

During the last month, Linda had been rather pestered. Holly Smith, Terry Moore and Alastair Dougal had also made offers that couldn't be refused to Brendan, Maureen and Brian O'Flaherty. 'He's not ready to do anything yet,' she told Thelma and Patrick. 'But I'll try.'

Next Saturday, Sarah and James kept their promise and the trek set off to Beacon Hill. Linda kept hers by taking Daniel Emanuel for a walk in Weavers Close. But it was one of Daniel Emanuel's saintly days. Nothing happened, except that Mrs Platt saw them and hurried out saying, 'Little children like you oughtn't to be out alone!' She brought them inside the cottage, where it was neat and plain and brown, and made them sit down. Linda looked hopefully round for biscuits at least, but Mrs Platt sat down too and told them the story of Jesus. Linda knew it. She had been sent home from school on her first day crying about Jesus. She turned paler and paler.

'Did it hurt much?' she whispered.

'What, dear?' asked Mrs Platt.

'Being nailed up in a tree,' Linda whispered.

Mrs Platt was rather taken aback. 'Well –' Since she did not quite know what to tell Linda, she took them back home feeling she had given them both something to think about.

She had. While Mrs O'Flaherty was trying to stop Linda crying, Daniel Emanuel collected four nails, a hammer and some string, and marched off to the oak-tree in the football field to find out for himself if it hurt to be crucified.

Luckily for him, he got tangled in the string before he had banged in the first nail properly. Even more luckily, Sarah, James, Patrick and Thelma happened to be coming home only an hour later than that after an almost perfect day. They heard the thin little wailing, which was all the noise Daniel Emanuel was able to make by then. 'That's Daniel Emanuel!' said Thelma, and managed to make Chunter gallop. And it was lucky the ponies were there. Daniel Emanuel was quite high up, hanging mostly by one arm. They managed to reach him by putting the ponies under the branch and James standing on the ponies, one foot on Chunter and one on Ben, boosting Patrick to the branch to cut the string. Sarah held the ponies and Thelma caught Daniel Emanuel as he came down. He hurt a lot, and he was frozen, and he was very angry. 'It's not *good* for people!' he kept saying as he rode home in front of Thelma. They put him to bed, and he brooded. He was very angry with both the Platts. They pretended to be kind and told you bad things.

Mr and Mrs Platt went from house to house with a petition to have the oak-tree cut down. They said it was very dangerous.

'Wouldn't it be easier to take Daniel Emanuel to the vet?' Mrs Willis asked sweetly.

Mr Platt didn't follow her meaning at all; but he followed Mr O'Flaherty's meaning when Mr O'Flaherty told him what to do with his petition.

Daniel Emanuel was still brooding. 'He's nearly ready,' Linda told the others. Nearly every day, Daniel Emanuel went round to Weavers Close and stood looking at the cottage thinking what to do. If Mr and Mrs Platt came out to take him home, he had vanished when they got to the road. But one day the Platts went out in their car. Daniel Emanuel wandered through the garden and round the back. He wandered thoughtfully through all the greenhouses. Mr Platt had never stopped building greenhouses. There were six by now. Daniel Emanuel ate tomatoes in one and picked a bunch of flowers in two. He made pies in flowerpots in the other three, thinking, thinking. But none of it gave him any ideas and he went away.

Mr Platt did not want to meet Mr O'Flaherty face to face again. He telephoned and pointed out Daniel Emanuel was being allowed to run wild. It was not so much the tomatoes, he said, but the child's own good . . . The person the other end rang off. 'Will you come here, Danny!' Mr O'Flaherty roared.

Mr Platt would have been shocked at the storm which broke out then.

When it was over, Mr O'Flaherty went out in a car to cool down. Mrs O'Flaherty lay down and read *The Count of Monte Cristo* to calm her nerves. Daniel Emanuel, very sore and sullen, went to watch television.

It was a programme about birds. The hen-bird came tiptoeing on to the screen, thin and brown and nervy, jerking its little head in just the same way that Mrs Platt did when she explained something for your own good. The cock-bird strutted on and bent its neck back just like Mr Platt. Then it spread out a great circle of tail and looked exactly like Mr Platt admiring a greenhouse.

'Platt, Platt!' shrieked Daniel Emanuel and ran to find Linda.

Linda was cooking. She had tipped in a bag of flour and a bag of sugar and she was trying to crunch in a dozen eggs with a fork before Mrs O'Flaherty stopped reading and found her. 'I'm busy,' she said. But her sleeve was being pulled in a particular way. She went with Daniel Emanuel and a trail of flour and mashed eggshell and looked at the television. 'Peacocks,' she said.

'Platts,' Daniel Emanuel said. He went into the front garden among the pieces of car and thought of a peacock. When the peacock came, it was blue and green and trailed its tail like a filmstar's skirt. It stood in front of a shiny hubcap in a piece of car and looked at itself and admired itself greatly. Daniel Emanuel nodded and thought of a peahen. She tiptoed up like Mrs Platt going after somebody's stray pet. Daniel Emanuel nodded again. 'Peacocks,' he murmured. 'Hundreds and hundreds.' And he thought of himself holding open a gap in the hedge behind Mr Platt's greenhouses to let a long, long line of peacocks and peahens tiptoe through. Hundreds, hundreds . . .

When Mrs O'Flaherty had finished dealing with Linda, she

165

was very relieved to find Daniel Emanuel curled up asleep beside the hubcap of a piece of car. 'Oh, isn't he an angel!' she said.

And the Platts were suddenly overwhelmed with peacocks. They sat in rows on the cottage roof, and the garden was a mass of tiptoeing green and brown, mixed with spreading tails and horrible sudden peacock screams. Peacocks got in the greenhouses. They invaded the house . . . But long before this, Holly Smith had rushed home shouting the news. Mrs Smith telephoned everyone in Chipping Hanbury and all the adults promptly pretended to be ill and sent their children to the football field. Mrs Willis gave up typing for other people and typed instead the news brought by a stream of children on bicycles. James and Sarah cantered from house to house delivering little cryptic notes saying things like: TWO MORE FELL THROUGH THE GREENHOUSES, and SHE GOT PECKED, and DROPPINGS ALL OVER SOFA, and ONE LAID AN EGG IN THEIR LOO, and ROOSTING ON TELEPHONE WHEN THEY TRIED TO RING VET.

A row of interested heads watched over the hedge when the Platts tried to get their car out and drive a load of peacocks to the vet. The running, the chasing, the shooing, the squawks and clouds of feathers were quite indescribable. Mrs Willis's note summed it up: THEY COULDN'T. So Mr Platt tried going round all the houses asking for help. The peacocks seemed fond of him. Twenty or so followed him faithfully from door to door and drowned his voice with screams when the doors were opened. Mr Platt was sorry to find that everyone opened the door wearing nightclothes and holding a handkerchief to their faces. There seemed to be quite a flu epidemic. So he went home, followed by his procession of birds, and the Platts waited for the peacocks to go away. But they didn't. If anything, they seemed to get more every day.

The Platts stood it for almost a month and then they went away themselves. Everyone recovered from flu in time to wave goodbye to their car as it drove off with peacocks clinging to the roof-rack and more hastily waddling and flapping behind. Linda had a marvellous time that day. Mrs O'Flaherty was touched and puzzled at the way everyone seemed to be thinking of treats for Linda and Daniel Emanuel.

The Platts' cottage is still standing empty except for peacocks, but some of the peacocks seem to have lost interest and wandered away. Since then there have been outbreaks of peacocks here and there all round the edges of London. This is because Daniel Emanuel has forgotten about them. He has started school now and has other things to think of.

GLIDOGRAM SOLUTIONS

Obvious: 1. Cents 2. Error 3. Naked 4. Teeth 5. Untie 6. Robot 7. Idiot 8. Erase 9. Swift
Centuries last a hundred years.

Proverbial: 1. Ears 2. Adam's 3. Bread 4. Bones 5. Sword 6. Enemy 7. Birds 8. Knave 9. Eggs
A drowning man will clutch at a straw.

THE LAST MAGICIAN

Peter Dickinson

A hundred miles beyond Beyond,
  Nearer than Here, further than Far,
The last magician breaks his wand
  And shapes the splinters to a star.

Then, leaning in the door of death,
  With his last art he forms a spark,
Breathes on it with his dying breath
  And leaves it flaming in the dark.

A planet circles round that star.
  There Life evolves, and men who learn
The secretest of things, and are
  Master magicians in their turn.

A hundred ages pass. The sun
  Begins to die. The wizards' skill
Makes hideous weapons. One by one
  They hunt and slay each other, till,

A hundred miles beyond Beyond,
  Nearer than Here, further than Far,
The last magician breaks his wand
  And shapes the splinters to a star.

We hope you have enjoyed this book.

There are more than 1,000 Puffins to choose from, and some are described on the following pages.

THE CRACK-A-JOKE BOOK

Another very special kind of book, not only because it was the thousandth Puffin, but because it was collected by children *for* children.

Famous people, like the Goodies, invited children from all over Great Britain to send in their favourite jokes; artists Mahood and Gerry Downes did the illustrations for love, and Penguin Books donated all profits to Oxfam to help children in need all over the world.

I LIKE THIS POEM

edited by Kaye Webb

The International Year of the Child was only meant to last for 1979, but it has lasted a lot longer through projects like this special book. It is a unique selection of poetry, chosen by children for other children who may be deprived of material things as well as poetry, and royalties are donated to The International Year of the Child.

A NECKLACE OF RAINDROPS AND OTHER STORIES

Joan Aiken

Many impossible things seem easy with an imagination and a storytelling power like Joan Aiken's, and never more so than in this collection of beautiful, scintillating, magical, poetical dreams and fancies which are very like the necklace of raindrops in the title story.

DOG DAYS AND CAT NAPS

Gene Kemp

Ten stories about animals – and their human owners. Cats and dogs are particularly prominent, but mice, gerbils and other assorted animals also weave their way through this delightfully off-beat collection.

THE GOOD BOOK GUIDE TO CHILDREN'S BOOKS

* Recommends over 500 books selected from 52 different publishers, 50% of them paperbacks, for children of 0 to 12.

* Completely revised and updated to include the latest fiction and non-fiction from bright, colourful picture books to computer books and classics.

* Designed for parents and children to use, separately or together

Heard about the Puffin Club?

. . . it's a way of finding out more about Puffin books and authors, of winning prizes (in competitions), sharing jokes, a secret code, and perhaps seeing your name in print! When you join you get a copy of our magazine, *Puffin Post*, sent to you four times a year, a badge and membership book.

For details of subscription and an application form, send a stamped addressed envelope to:

> *The Puffin Club Dept A*
> *Penguin Books Limited*
> *Bath Road*
> *Harmondsworth*
> *Middlesex* UB7 ODA

and if you live in Australia, please write to:

> *The Australian Puffin Club*
> *Penguin Books Australia Limited*
> *P.O. Box 257*
> *Ringwood*
> *Victoria 3134*